Love Me

C. J. Collins

Contents

Chapter - 1

♥

Sometimes it's better to let go because holding on hurts more.

Eugene stared at the mesmerizing ball of red that painted the skies in different hues of orange. The blowing evening sea breeze ruffled his dark locks and whipped over his flawless skin in a gentle caress. The ocean water shimmered, reflecting the colors of the sky that blended so beautifully with its vibrant blue.

He inhaled the notes of salt and the symphony of waves that tried to soothe the ache in his heart. The tranquility should have been everything Eugene once wanted. It was his favorite thing in the world. He once used to tell his close ones that five minutes at the beach was all he needed to unwind.

The waves would kiss his feet, removing all his pain and worries. But even that wasn't enough today. His chest constricted, and his breathing shallow as the heaviness in his heart only grew.

"Do you not want this child?" His best friend Dan's voice pulled him out of his thoughts. "You always wanted to be a father. I thought this would make you happy."

The earlier birthday celebration and the announcement of his pregnancy had been everything Eugene ever wanted. A few years ago, if someone asked what his dream was, he'd proudly answer that he wanted to become a homemaker and raise as many children as possible. He still did, somewhere in the dingy corner of his heart.

"Eugene?" Dan called worriedly and immediately shifted an inch closer before lifting a hand to brush his cheeks. Eugene hadn't even realized he was crying until he saw the wetness on Dan's fingers.

"It hurts," he admitted out loud for the world to hear for the first time since his wedding.

"Your stomach?" Dan's scent shifted with worry, and his hand dropped to cup Eugene's stomach. "We should go to the doctor. Come on." He moved to stand, but Eugene shook his head with a sad smile.

"My heart, Tae. My heart is hurting."

Dan frowned. "What? What happened? I thought you were happy." He moved in front of him, blocking the view of the ocean. "Is he a prick? Does he not treat you well?"

Eugene hung his head. "I wish," he whispered. That was the problem. His husband was the sweetest man in the world. Ryan Miller was the husband of everyone's dreams of having but couldn't have. He was respectful and caring. Soft-spoken and gentle. He was always considerate. But—

"Then why?"

There is no love.

Eugene lifted his head to lock his gaze on Dan. "He doesn't love me."

Carrying that not-so-secret in his heart had weighed him down for these two years. The feeling only got worse after he admitted it out loud. Eugene didn't know if it was even possible to hear his heart breaking, but he did.

Ryan never loved him and would never love him. The alpha only had one person in his heart, and that person wasn't Eugene. His kind and gentle eyes would never look at him with an emotion that he longed to see in them.

He sensed how the crack in his heart grew until it shattered into several million pieces—a crushing feeling of anguish and despair flooding his chest. The last time he felt this way was when he lost his twin, Ethan—his other half.

Growing up, they had always been thick as thieves, always attached to their hips. They were inseparable and even dreamed of mating the same alpha or alpha twins so they wouldn't be apart.

But fate was cruel. When the first blossoms of love bloomed in their heart simultaneously, it also came with a startling realization that only one would win. And that was Ethan.

Ryan Miller, the tall and handsome alpha introduced to them by their parents in a social gathering, won their attention from the first second, but the alpha had his eyes only on one. Six months of whirlwind courting led to the most beautiful wedding on the planet.

The Miller family had settled in the US for decades and had their business there. They were only in Spain for a few months to set up a subsidiary to stay connected with their roots. And they were even happier that their son found a mate from Spain.

Ethan broke their promise for the first time when he decided he wanted to live overseas with his alpha. His twin didn't even stop to apologize or offer soothing words to the other. He was too drunk in his love for his alpha.

And just like that, Ethan was gone, leaving Eugene alone to navigate the world all by himself. They continued to keep in touch, but most of the calls involved Ethan gushing over his alpha and talking about his relationship.

It was dreamy—everything they ever wanted for themselves. Eugene was happy in his world, but love was painful. His omega understood they could never have the alpha as soon as they realized they had imprinted on him.

The giddiness that came with identifying Ryan as their potential mate waned when the wolf and human noticed how the alpha's gaze was locked on a blushing Ethan. Their scents bloomed and mingled with each other's possessions. They had chosen each other.

So Eugene had respectfully stepped back, swallowing the pain that came with the first rejection. It hadn't been even that long, but it was enough to leave an everlasting dent in his heart. Even then, his heart was only crushed. But now it was broken.

"But Ryan—"

"Ethan is the only one in his heart." Eugene took a shuddering breath because even that hurt. The ache in his chest had spread to his entire body. Even a simple movement hurts now.

"T-That cannot be true," Dan whispered. "I've seen the way he looks at you. H-He—"

Eugene leaned to cup the omega's face with both his hands. "Look at me," he commanded. When he did, Eugene saw how Dan swallowed, his eyes blinking slowly. "What do you see?" To be more specific. "Who do you see?" his voice cracked, and he dared not utter another word.

He felt Dan tense under his palms. He smelled his sweet apple cinnamon scent sour a little. Eugene knew what he would see—silver hair, blue eyes, a small button nose, and plush lips. Silver hoops adorned both his ears, and he wore chains and rings that his twin once cherished.

"J-Ethan." Dan silently cursed under his breath. His friend was sharp, and it didn't take any more words to convey his turmoil.

Eugene dropped his hands with a sad chuckle and fixed his sorrowful eyes on the gentle waves. Oh, how much he wished his life was simple. How much he wished he could go back in time and change things.

If only his twin hadn't been so selfish. Ethan would often tell him he was so happy he could die. And he did that not even a year later, once again breaking his promises entirely.

Ethan was already pregnant when they married. Only seven months after their wedding, Ethan gave birth to a beautiful boy—an alpha pup. The family was ecstatic. Eugene was there to witness the happy couple, cradling the bundle of joy in their arms.

It was then Eugene was trying to heal and move on. He'd come to peace with his feelings and was going on dates, talking to alphas, trying to find the one. He even met a kind alpha and thought he could find his happiness.

But then it all came crashing down with that one terrifying phone call. Ethan was killed on the spot in a horrible road accident. His car had collided head-on with an oncoming truck.

Ryan was broken with a two-month-old pup, who didn't even know his dada was no more. The upcoming events were still a blur for Eugene. He, himself, had been numb throughout the entirety of the funeral and had trouble processing the information.

He'd felt a searing pain as if his heart had been ripped apart when it happened, and his wolf went silent for over a week. Perhaps it sensed the loss of their other half.

The pup was inconsolable and stopped crying only when Eugene held him. Maybe it was because their scents were somewhat similar or because of their uncanny resemblance. They were identical, after all.

To his family, seeing him in flesh and blood next to Ethan's photo was bitter sweat. Ryan wouldn't even look in his direction. Eugene hadn't despised his existence so much until that moment. He understood because he couldn't see his face either.

But then his entire focus was on the pup, who kept nuzzling into his chest for milk. Eugene's maternal instincts kicked in, and the love for his nephew had taken a front seat. In their world, a pup didn't last long without his mother. So Eugene took it upon himself to take care of the pup, who refused to consume anything if it wasn't him who was feeding him.

With the doctor's suggestion, Eugene changed his hair color, setting him apart from his twin to become part of the pup's world. But that had soon become the bane of his existence. Soon, his grief-ridden mother began to see him as Ethan, even calling him by his name.

His father and grandmother suggested ridiculously that he marry Ryan because it was best for the pup. Eugene knew it was the worst idea ever, but when Ryan had only nodded and said nothing else, he'd lost the battle.

He could only think about the pup in his hands and how he couldn't see him suffer. Eugene welcomed the pain knowingly. But nothing had prepared him for the actual move. Moving into his twin's home was one thing, but seeing everything that was part of his life was a painful reminder.

He and Ryan were treading on eggshells around each other until nature slowly took its course. They fell into a comfortable pace, bonding over the pup. They were a great team, and they worked so well.

Their laughter and joy were sometimes contagious, but only because of the pup. Personally, they were still seven seas apart. That was all they would ever be.

Once again, Eugene had made peace with it. This was all his life would ever be, and love wasn't in the cards for him. But his treacherous heart once again betrayed him, falling head on heels for the alpha, who was also now his husband.

Every interaction brought them unintentionally closer, and Eugene hadn't expected to spend the alpha's rut with him. But he'd been weak. He couldn't resist him or fight against the feelings for so long. He'd finally succumbed and gave in.

The heated kisses and lingering touches, hot and passionate love-making, were still fresh in his mind. But so was the moment that shattered the illusion. After years, Eugene finally felt treasured, desired, and wanted. Touched in a way he always dreamed of being touched. Taken in a way he longed for.

But then, just a few seconds before knotting him for one last time, Ryan had whispered his twin's name. The omega opened his eyes with a startling realization, hot pain searing through his chest as the alpha's tears wet his skin, teeth digging into his shoulders and hips stuttering with his release.

Ryan hadn't once addressed him by his name since the start of his rut. The truth was like a hard ball clogging his throat. The omega had choked on a sob, the alpha too out of it to notice how his scent grew bitter.

He'd slipped out of bed as soon as the knot had deflated, scrubbing his body in the shower with tears rolling down his cheeks as he struggled to breathe. The pain was fresh and too much to bear. As he stood under the shower, watching the remnants of their passion wash down the drain, Eugene also realized Ryan had never called him by his name that often.

To make things worse, they'd returned to their old pace after that. No one brought the four days of passion into each other's embrace. There were no more touches, no more warm smiles. It felt as if Ryan was avoiding him altogether if it wasn't to talk about the pup.

Eugene once again had made peace with the fact. It was his mistake, after all. He should have pushed the alpha away and stopped him from crossing the boundaries. Instead, he'd whimpered and melted in his arms when their lips touched. He'd been desperate for those touches, just like Ryan was. He just hadn't been ready for the pain that would follow.

The following weeks had been painful and reminded Eugene that he would always be a replacement for Ethan. He was in the Miller household only because he shared his face and other features with his late brother. Things only worsened when he saw Ryan going through albums, reminiscing his memories of Ethan with their pup.

Usually, Eugene didn't take it to heart when his mom slipped and called him Ethan. He took consolation, knowing his mom took comfort in him. However, it was a nail on the chalkboard whenever she did that now. It had been two years, yet she couldn't move on from his brother.

The silence between him and Dan had stretched, allowing him to be lost in his thoughts. His friend settled beside him and stared at the sea. Dan's thumb caressed the back of his hand, and Eugene just sat staring at the sea. No words were exchanged. The silence had never been this heavy between them.

It was his birthday today. His parents have flown to the US, and the Millers have come over to celebrate. On the table was a giant cake along with Ethan's photo. To Eugene, it was a painful reminder of the years he had celebrated with his twin.

The moment was great, and their happiness doubled when Ryan announced that Eugene was expecting. Everyone took turns in congratulating Eugene. However, he couldn't rejoice. His child wasn't born out of both parents' love. It was a result of his momentary weakness and its other father's desperation.

When he found out a few weeks ago, he was very nervous, not knowing how to tell Ryan. But he'd have to. Not like he could hide this. So, after dinner, he slid the test result silently toward the alpha. Ryan had been silent for a long moment—too long for Eugene's liking. He was ready for the bomb to drop, but Ryan, the sweetest alpha he was, had told him he'd take responsibility and do whatever it took to make it comfortable for him.

What could he do? He nodded silently again as he did several million other times and muttered good night before excusing himself from the table. Ryan always did the dishes at night, and Eugene helped. But that night, Eugene didn't bother. The heaviness in his heart was too much to bear.

Dan, his best friend, who had also flown from Spain to spend this birthday with him, pulled him aside to talk. The Miller family owned a beach guest house where they had assembled for the occasion. It was Ryan's idea to break the news to them during the celebration, and Eugene went along with it.

With the pup spending time with his grandparents, Eugene slipped away with Dan to get a much-needed breather. Eugene had swallowed it all for years and pretended everything was fine. But today, it was all overwhelming.

"I miss me," he said, breaking the silence. The sky was gray now, with the last hues of orange disappearing from the horizon. "I don't even remember the old me anymore. It feels like I'm staring at someone else and living their life instead of mine. Do you know even Mom calls me Ethan these days and doesn't bother correcting it? Dad...I'm not sure."

His father became withdrawn after losing Ethan. Between the two, his father had always been fond of Ethan. Eugene didn't even want to go there. They didn't talk much.

"Why didn't you tell me?" Dan's voice was pained. "Why are you doing this to yourself?"

"I wish I had the right answer." Eugene smiled sadly. "At first, Ethan's pup was my responsibility. Then, it became my duty. I thought I could handle my feelings for Ryan and being married to him, but I was so wrong."

"I told you it was a bad idea." His friend's voice was defeated.

Dan tried to talk him out of the wedding but failed. Eugene had been adamant and believed it was the right thing to do. He never considered what this could do to his heart.

Eugene shrugged. "I want to tell you I had no choice, but it was a conscious decision. I promised Ethan I'd always be there for him. He isn't here anymore, but I couldn't let his pup suffer. The doctor said the pups that lose their mother at an early stage often don't make it. I was afraid and wouldn't have forgiven myself if something happened to him. But now, I don't think I can do this anymore."

The pup had to be admitted to the hospital following Ethan's death because the effects of losing the maternal bond were too painful for the pup. When it became evident it would be hard for him to survive without that bond, the doctors recommended trying it out with Eugene. He had volunteered wholeheartedly and without any regrets. "What do you plan to do?" Dan asked, no judgment in his tone, only concern. "What do I do to take this pain away?"

"You can't do anything," Eugene replied. "I don't know what to do with myself either."

"You can go somewhere for a while," His friend suggested. "Get away from all this. You know you haven't been to Spain in ages. You could take a mini vacation. Aron is old enough to stay with his grandparents and doesn't ask for you much these days."

That was another painful reminder Eugene didn't need. Ryan's parents often took him to spend time with him, saying he needed to bond with his family. It was usually once a week, but now it has become a few days a week.

When he was there, Ryan always went there from the office. Some nights, he came home, and other nights, he stayed at his parent's place with the pup. Eugene sometimes thought they didn't really need him anymore. His job was done. The pup was alive and healthy now.

"Or you can go with me to Italy. I'll be there for a few months."

Eugene shook his head. "I don't know, Dan." Leaving wasn't as easy as it sounded. He couldn't leave just like that. Or could he? The pup still needed him, didn't he? Even if it was as little as he used to ask for him before. These days, the pup didn't need anyone if Ryan was there.

"Take your time, but if you need a break, you know the choice is always there. Maybe it'll give you some clarity." Dan's words were convincing. "Ethan's death was as hard for you as everyone else. I'd say it's even more because you've never been apart until his wedding. He wasn't just your brother but also your best friend."

Eugene sniffled. "It is what it is. Everyone is so focused on their hurt that they forget I exist." Saying it out loud was liberating but also painful. He often wondered if he was imagining things or if Eugene really ceased to exist in their eyes. Dan checked the time. "Come on. I need to leave in a few. They might be looking for you."

Eugene took his hand and allowed his friend to lift him.

"This isn't over. You don't look the same anymore, Eugene. I'm not talking about appearance," Dan exasperated. "You look dead. It's not the Eugene I used to know. I wanted to ask you many times, but you kept assuring me you were alright. Then you said you spent the rut with him. I thought things were changing."

A ball of emotion closed his throat again.

"If this is how things are, then we need to talk. I refuse to let you be sad. We will figure out a way. Don't bury all these things inside you. It's not good."

Eugene nodded. With a sigh, he took Dan's hand. "Don't tell anyone."

"You don't have to tell me that, Eugene. You know I always take your side." The gentle squeeze was assuring, and he was happy to hear his name repeated.

Dan hugged him, and Eugene sank into his embrace, soaking up all the comfort, discreetly wiping his tears. His mind was in turmoil, and he saw no end to it. For now, he'd just take this comfort and worry about it later.

***

"What happened to your hair?!"

"Why did you do this?"

Eugene glanced up at his mom and mother-in-law, who talked at the same time as soon as he entered the dining hall for breakfast. He combed his fingers through his freshly dyed black hair with a soft smile. "Just missed my original color."

He sat at the table beside Ryan, who was blatantly staring at him but hadn't said anything. The pup was on his lap. Eugene leaned to press a kiss on his temple, but the pup stared at him before turning his head away to bury his face into Ryan's chest.

Eugene felt a pang in his chest but masked it with a smile. He settled to ruffle his hair instead and grabbed a plate.

"I preferred silver," Ryan's mom said.

His mom had gone silent and pushed the food around her plate as if seeing him was too much for her. Eugene forced himself to spoon some gravy onto his plate to mask the awkward silence that followed his appearance.

Ryan's father started to talk about something else, and while Eugene was glad for the topic change, it didn't mean everything was alright.

He tried to engage with the pup a few times but he turned away, clinging to his alpha father even more. Eugene swallowed his rising sadness and pretended everything was fine. He was now an expert at it.

After breakfast, however, Ryan's mom stopped him. "Change your hair color to silver. You noticed how uncomfortable everyone was. What is the need to do this now? Everything was going fine, wasn't it?"

Eugene stared at her in disbelief. He sucked in a sharp breath.

"Peter will take you to the spa here. He knows all the places. Go and change it first."

"What's wrong with this color?" he asked, almost offended.

She stared at him, nostrils flaring. "Everything," she hissed. "You saw how the pup reacted. He thinks you're a stranger. That's not good."

Eugene notched his chin, swallowing the sob that wanted out. "But I'm a stranger," he huffed. "I'm not Ethan."

"What's wrong with you?!" she hissed, glancing around quickly and lowering her voice. "Are you trying to stir drama now? Do you think I don't know that? You could never match his elegance no matter how hard you try," she scoffed. "You already got what you want. You have my son's attention and my grandpup's. What more? You're pregnant. Things are finally falling into place, and you're kicking fuss over something so trivial? Don't forget you're here because of Ethan. My son loves only him. Not you."

Eugene couldn't stop the tears well up in his eyes from falling down his cheeks. "I'm aware."

"Good. Be a good omega. Go and change your hair color. Stop pulling these stunts. It doesn't look good in public. If the media caught you like this, they're gonna write articles about it," she hissed, and everything else was just a buzz for Eugene.

I'm not wanted here.

They don't need me.

They want Ethan. Not me.

It wasn't like he could forget how they stopped his public appearances after the few leaked photos and articles about the Miller family finding a replacement for their son-in-law only months after losing him.

To make things worse, later that day, he walked in on his mother talking excitedly to his in-laws. "I wish this pup was an omega. He or she would look just like my Ethan. It's like Ethan himself is going to be born again, don't you think?"

Eugene couldn't bear it anymore. Wiping the silent tears, he returned to his room without further words. Perhaps making a decision while being emotional wasn't a great idea. But Eugene had decided. There was no turning back now.

When everyone else was busy downstairs, he packed silently in his room, recalling how no one was surprised to see the couple used separate rooms, how Ryan's mother had even arranged it before his arrival. Everything was clear now.

He was still an outsider in this family. Someone who was allowed to stay because of his resemblance to the actual member of the family, Ethan. To console a pup who needed his omega father and an alpha who was still madly in love with his late mate. To put up appearances in front of the public.

That night, when everyone was asleep, he left without looking back. He had no destination in mind but just knew he couldn't stay here any longer, not like this. He couldn't lose himself and refused to bring his pup into a loveless marriage.

He left a letter before his brother's photo adorned with fresh flowers. His smile was frozen in time. Eugene remembered that photo. After all, he was the one behind the camera. It was the first photo he sent to Ryan to save as a contact image.

Eugene swallowed thickly and strengthened his resolve. The path ahead of him was uncertain but offered some hope. Maybe the pain won't be much worse.

"Bye, Ethan... as much as I love you, I have to let you go. I can't let your memories hold me back. I can't let them do this to me anymore," he whispered before pivoting on his heels, ignoring the confused security and getting into a cab he rented. The car whirred past the several mansions in that area, the ocean growing further with every second. And Eugene... didn't look back.

***

The next day, the staff found the letter first. One by one, the members of the household were informed. *It read:*

Maybe I'm a coward for leaving like this, but I had no energy to face you all again, knowing that the person you're looking for in me is Ethan and not Eugene.

Ryan, thank you for treating me well and with respect. I know you're still in love with my brother, and I'll never be able to fill his shoes. Trust me. I tried. I became someone I wasn't, yet it wasn't enough. I cannot do this anymore. Your pup doesn't need me anymore, and I have fulfilled my promise to my brother, even though he broke every single one he made. This is as far as we go.

There are days I wish God had taken me instead of my brother. But what happened cannot simply be undone or erased. You can't pretend I'm Ethan. He's gone forever and isn't coming back. Perhaps it was easy to pretend that he was still here, but the truth is that he's not here.

I wish you to heal and move on in the direction you want to take from here. But I cannot be a part of that journey. Once again, thank you for all your kindness during the time we have known each other.

Mom, I'm not Ethan. Hope you don't miss me too much because Eugene is gone for a while now from your mind. Guess you forgot all about me with Ethan taking up all your thoughts. Maybe this way, you will miss me more. It might sound cruel coming from me, but I can't be Ethan anymore. Eugene needed you too.

I never complained when he took up all my space or drew all attention to himself since childhood. I never complained when you wanted me to take his place in his family and play pretend for the sake of his pup. I never complained when all of you overlooked my pain and loss and behaved as if everything was fine.

You forgot I loved him too. We shared a womb and were never apart. I tried to be understanding of your grief, but I was grieving too. Unlike you, I was grieving the loss of both Ethan and Eugene. In your eyes, Eugene stopped existing the day Ethan died. You all kept searching for him in me that you forgot I'm a person too. One with feelings and emotions and that I get hurt too.

Yesterday, Ryan's mother kindly reminded me that I was here only because I looked like Ethan. Thank you very much. I needed it. Because I was beginning to lose sight of who I was. Ethan and I always had different tastes and preferences. We were so alike yet so different.

When my pup is born, I want him or her to look like me, Eugene Sanchez. I don't know what is waiting for us or how arduous this journey might be, but I'm determined to see this through and ensure no one ruins this for me.

I always wanted to marry for love. I don't regret my choice, but I will regret it if I stay any longer.

I had too many dreams, and I gave that all up to play this role I never wanted but was forced to by the situation. Now, I don't see the need for it anymore. Everyone is doing fine, and seriously, I don't think anyone would even miss me.

You will always be in my thoughts, no matter how far I am. Maybe someday we can meet again under better circumstances. Until then... let me be.

- Eugene

Chapter - 2

♥

"**P**romise me."

Ryan blinked slowly, tearing his gaze from one spectacular view in front of him to the other. Ethan looked exquisite with the morning rays of the sun providing a healthy glow to his skin. His night robe slid down one shoulder, exposing the flawless skin that was littered with his marks. His cheeks were flushed pink from a recent hot shower. Eyes narrowed at him with a pout forming on his lips.

Beautiful.

Ryan couldn't help but lean forward to capture those plump lips between his teeth, nibbling it, earning a soft sigh from his Omega. "What promise?"

"That you'll never forget me," Ethan said earnestly. "Promise me I'm the only omega in your life."

Ryan chuckled, playing with his delicate fingers. "We're married, sweetheart. I'm already yours, and you're mine."

"No." Ethan pouted. "That's not enough. I want you to promise me."

Ryan rolled his eyes at the silliness. He hooked Ethan's ring finger with his. "This is my promise." His gaze flicked to their rings. "There's only one omega in my life, and that's you."

Ethan beamed before throwing a leg over his hip to straddle him. The night robe moved, revealing his smooth legs. Ryan let out an appreciative hum, immediately trailing his hands over that buttery smoothness.

"Not enough." Ethan kissed him breathlessly. "Even if something happened to me and gone, I want to be the only omega in your life," he demanded, warm breath fanning his lips. "I won't forgive you if you ever looked at another." His voice rang with a possessiveness Ryan was used to.

"Why do you have to say something like that?" Ryan growled, rolling them to pin him under him. "You know I hate it when you say shit like that."

"What? About being the only Omega in your life?" Ethan quirked his brows. "You don't want to move on already?" His scent flared with irritation.

Ryan frowned. "I don't like you being pessimistic all the time. What's with this? Aren't we happy? Didn't we promise forever with each other?"

Ethan sighed. "Ryan, I'm just saying I love you so much that even if you die, I'll never move on. I won't be able to. You'll be the only one for me. I want us to meet in our next life and all our other lives after that."

Ryan huffed a breath. Ethan has always been like that. He didn't think it was possible to end this conversation without giving in. This entire thing was ridiculous. Why would he want to talk about death and what happens after when they are both alive and well? It was their honeymoon, for god's sake.

Not to mention, Ethan was carrying his pup. It frustrated his alpha to no extent when Ethan brought up something like this. He closed his eyes to pull in a deep breath.

"I promise," he said when he opened them. "There's only one Omega in my life, and that's you. Even in the worst-case scenario, it's not gonna change."

Ethan's sweet orange scent bloomed around him. "Thank you, alpha." He glanced up at him with a sultry look that stirred the heat in Ryan's belly. "So why don't we seal the promise then, hmm?"

Ryan was only happy to oblige, sighing in relief now that the crisis had been averted.

***

Ryan was numb. The sounds of the surroundings were only white noise, and the infant's cries in his arms sounded too distant.

He was distraught and couldn't remove Ethan's bloodied and battered form, barely recognizable in the mortuary. The police had called to identify the victim of the morning accident.

Was there really a God? If there was one, then he was a cruel man. How could he do this to Ethan? How could he take his pup's father like that?

Ryan didn't know if he should be mourning the loss of his mate or try to calm his pup, who was crying for his omega father. The searing pain in his heart made it nearly impossible to breathe. He couldn't even imagine what was happening with his pup.

Hours blurred past until someone took the pup from his hands. His cries grew distant, but Ryan didn't move from the spot where his knees had given out. He didn't care that he was sitting in the same place where he'd wretched his guts out after witnessing the most horrible death in his life.

Ethan was gone. Once and for all. The smiling face he kissed that morning was no more.

***

"I'm sorry, Mr. Miller... less than ten percent of pups make it out alive in such cases. Aron is too young to survive without an omega parent. We are trying our best."

Ryan's world fell apart for the second time in a span of two days. He didn't know what was worse, losing his mate or waiting for his son to take his last breath.

"Stay strong for him."

Strength was the last thing he felt then. Once again, no one stopped him when he slid to the floor. Pain and grief were all he felt; it was too much to bear.

What should he do? He wanted to get as far from the pup as possible. His heart hurt seeing him suffer like that. Even his scent wasn't enough to comfort the pup.

He heard everyone talking around him, trying their best to comfort the pup. His mom was all over the place, trying everything she could ever imagine. The doctors had sedated the pup for a while, but not anymore, not only because it was bad for his health but also because he needed to be fed.

And Aron refused to take the powdered milk. His body rejected anything else they tried to force-feed him. He'd been awake for a while now; his cries seeped through the ajar door, haunting more than ever.

Only a few days ago, those cries would put a smile on Ryan's face. He'd coo at his pup, soothing him before taking him to his omega father for nursing.

Ryan buried his fingers in his hair and pulled, his body shaking with sobs as he listened to the painful wail of his pup. Death would have been far kinder. He'd rather prefer that than going through this.

However, suddenly, the cries stopped. Ryan's heart sank to the pit of his stomach. His head whipped up, expecting the worst, and a roar bubbled in his throat when he saw it.

Eugene stood there, cradling his son to his chest. His pup frantically nuzzled into his chest with whimpers. A nurse rushed to his side with a baby bottle, which Eugene took with a tight smile that didn't reach his eyes.

Then, like a miracle, Aron began to suckle from the bottle. The loud sounds echoed around the room. Ryan's body sagged with relief.

The silence for the first time in days was heavenly, and Eugene was the angel with his signature black hair and soft eyes. This time, Ryan could mourn his mate peacefully.

***

Death was cruel in many ways, especially untimely ones. The dead were gone but left the family and loved ones in shambles. The shock, followed by grief and pain, was unexplainable. Everyone went through the different stages of grief differently, and the pace at which they processed it all differed.

Ryan hasn't even crossed the first stage. He was still in denial. Then, the anger joined. During the funeral, he refused to bid goodbye or speak at all. He was furious at Ethan for leaving him in the middle like that.

How dare he? He promised forever. Each interaction they ever had kept replaying in his mind, especially when he was curled in his mate's nest in the dead of the night.

Ethan was a pessimistic prick who manifested his death. It felt almost cruel that he was still smiling in the photo while Ryan had lost it forever.

Why did you have to go? I told you I'd take you in the evening after work. Why did you have to drive?

Ryan kept lamenting and wondering if there was anything he could have done to prevent it, but there was no possible answer.

Aron refused to move away from Eugene. Stepping into the room was a painful reminder of what he lost. Eugene was a replica of Ethan. Even their scents were almost the same, and it was hard on his wolf.

He knew his mate was gone forever, but having a lookalike parading with the same scent wasn't helpful at all for his grieving process. Ryan could tell Eugene wasn't in an ideal position either. He was in pain too.

Ethan didn't talk about his twin often, but Ryan knew they were thick as thieves. They were always on a video call when Ryan wasn't there. Eugene always checked in on Ethan.

First good mornings and good nights always came from Eugene. Even he was always the first to wish Ethan on every special occasion, including his birthday.

"I wish you were the first to wish me." Ethan had pouted.

Ryan smiled fondly. "He's your wombmate. Stop pouting and answer his call."

"But—"

Ryan silenced him with a kiss because Ethan was salty after seeing a text from Eugene. "No buts. Just answer it already. He knows you read the text."

"Still...I was waiting for you to wish me first. Why did he have to go first?" Ethan complained, not so pleased with the greeting.

"Because he's your brother who has never been apart from you since conception," Ryan reasoned. "Be nice to him, sweetheart."

"I'm nice to him," Ethan grumbled, letting the phone go to his voicemail.

"No. You're not. While I enjoy your obsession with me, I also understand how important this day is to Eugene just as much as you. It's his birthday too, sweetheart. Shouldn't you wish him first? I'm not going anywhere. We can celebrate as much as you want later. What's this five-minute phone call gonna take you away from?"

Ethan sighed, answering the second call, and forced a smile. He greeted in a high-pitched voice, "Happy Birthday, my bubbly boo!"

Ryan shook his head with a smile while patiently waiting for his mate to finish with the call. Sometimes, it felt like Ethan was being unreasonably rude to Eugene, who was nothing but a ball of sunshine.

"My husband has prepared this wonderful surprise," Ethan gushed over the phone, trying to describe every minute detail in a matter of seconds.

Ryan took the phone from him, ignoring his protests. "Happy Birthday, Eugene. Wish you have a wonderful year ahead."

"Thanks, Ryan."

"Apologies, I kept Ethan occupied that he couldn't call you first." Ryan knew Ethan was too lost in the surprise he *had* prepared that he didn't even remember to call his brother until he called first. But it would only hurt Eugene if he knew the truth.

"It's okay." Eugene chuckled. *"I'm happy as long as he's happy. Thanks for making this day special for him."*

"Always. So, how is your birthday going? Any plans?"

"Dan dragged me out for a surprise birthday bash." He could sense the smile on his face as he heard the sounds in the background. *"He wants to spend the day together since it's my first birthday without Ethan by my side."* Ryan felt a sense of longing there and glanced at Ethan, who was happily clicking photos of the cake.

"Why don't you come over here for a few days?" he suggested. "I can book your tickets. I'm sure your brother would be delighted to have you here."

"Oh, it's okay," Eugene said. *"I'm coming next month for his delivery anyway. I'll see him then."*

"Alright, give me a moment. Did you cut your cake already?" Ryan asked.

"Not yet."

"Okay. Let's go on a video call then," Ryan said. "Ethan was waiting for you too." It was a lie and Ethan made a face. Ryan narrowed his eyes with a stern look.

"Really?" Eugene's voice pulsed with delight.

Although they were in different time zones, Ryan had arranged the surprise for Spain time so they could celebrate with their family.

"Yes." Ryan smiled, sad that Ethan ignored his brother on their special day. While he knew Ethan loved him dearly, his priorities had definitely shifted. Still, he thought he should pay attention to his brother.

Maybe this has always been their dynamic. He didn't know. Ethan always changed the topics if he were to ask about Eugene or his friends. He always kept their interactions centered around them for some reason.

So they went on a video call, cutting the cake simultaneously and making a wish. Eugene's smile was blinding that day, and Ryan smiled, knowing he had done something right. Maybe he should just become the bridge between the brothers. He *had* already *taken* Ethan away and wouldn't let them drift apart anymore.

*****

The labor was complicated, and Ethan again reminded him about the promise they made. Ryan chastised him for even thinking about it. But after a tense few hours, the pup was born healthy.

Eugene stayed by his brother's side until two weeks ago. Aron was now almost three months old. Perhaps that was the reason the pup found comfort in Eugene because Eugene was beside Ethan all the time, except for when Ryan was with him.

"Mr. Miller, Aron has shown great improvements this week, and he's feeding well." The doctor's words offered comfort and hope. However, Ryan sensed a but coming.

"What is it?"

"A pup creates a bond with its omega parent from the moment of inception. They're entirely dependent on them through the initial years until they become independent. Their inner wolf relies heavily on this bond as they slowly explore this world, which is why it becomes hard for them to survive without a mother."

Ryan nodded in understanding.

"No one can fill a mother's shoes. But Eugene is your mate's twin. They're almost one and the same. You know, identical twins always have similar scents and characteristics. Besides, you told me that Eugene has been with him since his birth until two weeks ago."

"Yes, that's right," Ryan replied.

"That must be the reason why the pup has identified Eugene as his maternal figure. I figure your mate smells similar to Eugene?"

Ryan swallowed. He did. Though they both had citrusy scents, they weren't the same. While Ethan smelled like sweet oranges, Eugene's scent was fresh, like lime. It wasn't easy to tell apart for someone who hadn't spent enough time with them.

"The pup is too young to differentiate the slightest changes in notes of the scents that set the twins apart. Even then, it's not easy if they spend a lot of time together. Their scents would naturally blend with each other."

Ryan nodded in understanding.

"We recommend you leave the pup in Eugene's care until he's old enough. I understand it's a huge sacrifice to ask from an unmated omega, but his chances are higher if you can arrange this."

Ryan looked down at his hands. It was too much to ask Eugene. His life was in Spain, and if he wasn't wrong, he was dating someone. How could he ask him to take care of his son? It was such a cruel thing to do.

However, not asking meant he would have to watch his son wither away. Ryan was torn. He had already lost to Ethan. He couldn't lose the pup too. His wolf rattled inside his chest, whining at him.

In the end, the paternal instincts in him won, and he found himself nodding. He was ready to sacrifice anything in order to keep his pup alive. Perhaps they could come to some sort of mutual arrangement for a few years until his pup learned to be independent.

***

Ryan was wrong. He didn't know when or how the marriage talks began. Only two weeks after the doctor's visit, he and Eugene signed the legal papers at the court.

With this marriage, Eugene officially adopted Aron and became his parent. He still didn't understand why Eugene would agree to marry him. It made no sense when his mother said this was the only way and that Eugene's parents had already agreed.

Why didn't Eugene oppose? He even went to talk to Eugene, but the Omega was clear in his decision. "I'm doing this for Ethan," he had said. "I owe him that."

Ryan was dumbfounded. "This marriage will only be on paper. I can't be your husband outside of it. I can't forget him."

"I don't expect that." Eugene took a deep breath. "We are doing this for Aron. I'm sure we would make a great team."

"Team," Ryan whispered.

"Yes."

Ryan took a deep breath. What choice did he have? His son needed Eugene, and Eugene was willing to do this.

"What about your boyfriend? What does he say about all this?" he asked.

"We decided to part ways mutually," Eugene replied. "He understands."

Ryan stared at Eugene for a long moment. "I'll let you go when the time comes. I refuse to let you waste your life for the sake of my pup. Promise me you'll think about yourself too and won't be adamant about staying in this marriage for his sake."

Eugene's smile was sad, but he nodded. "I promise."

***

Things were said easier than done. They made a great team—a fantastic one if someone asked Ryan.

However, living together under the same roof and co-parenting a pup naturally brought them closer. With every passing month, Ryan was hurting a little less. The Omega radiated comfort, and Ryan took it.

Eugene was calm to his storm. He somehow anchored him and provided a sense of warmth. Ryan didn't know when his feelings toward the Omega began to change.

Eugene was so different from Ethan. They might have the same features, but Eugene was just that…Eugene.

While Ethan was sophisticated and molded to be a perfect socialite, Eugene was a free spirit who followed his heart. Ethan was so stringent about his diet and threw a fuss if there was even a slight difference in his calorie intake. Eugene laughed it off and hit the gym to get back into shape.

Eugene loved to paint, watch romantic comedies, and eat meat. He disliked cleaning or folding laundry but loved cooking and baking—more than anything, Eugene loved to read and had an entire collection in just a few months. In short, he was just an absolute delight to be around. He also became someone Ryan constantly needed.

While their home was still the same as Ethan left, Eugene's room was all him. Warm and welcoming. Ryan relished the moments he could go to his room; with time, he naturally wanted to spend more time in Eugene's room. He loved how their scents blended so well.

Ryan was falling, and he knew it. He didn't know if the time that passed was enough to heal his heart, but it wasn't hurting anymore when he saw Eugene. He didn't remember Ethan or see him in the Omega anymore. His wolf knew this Omega was different, though they looked alike.

However, the guilt of feeling that way was eating him alive. He didn't think it was the right thing to do. Eugene was here to help him with his pup. They were a great team.

Eugene never gave him any signs of his interest in him. What if Eugene wasn't feeling the same?

When Ryan somehow worked out the courage to move past that doubtful phase, his promise to Ethan returned to haunt him. Reliving his memories with Ethan was normal. He often has dreams of him.

However, that particular dream wrecked him and filled him with havoc. Ethan was gone, but he was thinking about another omega and craving to feel that warmth of love again.

Ryan couldn't meet Eugene's gaze in the following days. This was wrong. His wolf was disoriented.

"You promised me," Ethan's voice taunted every night. "It hasn't been even three years, but you've already moved on."

Ryan had whimpered in his sleep, apologizing to his Omega. It was so realistic that he felt himself crumbling.

"We were supposed to meet each other again in our next life."

Ryan woke in the cold, unable to dissociate reality from that of a dream.

"You lied."

"You don't love me anymore."

Ryan broke under pressure, shoulder racking with sobs. He was so lost and didn't know how to escape the pit of guilt.

He was spiraling, and he was spiraling fast. Just as he felt the waves enclosing him, wrapping around him and pulling him down forcefully, he heard Eugene's voice.

"Ryan? Oh, my god!"

Warm hands shook him, and sweet lime enveloped him. Suddenly, he could breathe again.

"Shit! You're cold." Eugene pulled the blankets hurriedly around his shoulders, rubbing his arms.

Ryan let out another sob, circling his hands around Eugene's waist. The Omega stiffened for a moment but relaxed before rubbing his back.

"It's alright. I got you," he whispered. "It's okay." He swayed them gently, staying with him as he slowly relaxed.

He was safe. Ryan buried his face into Eugene's chest, inhaling his scent and gulping it greedily. Eugene was his safe place. The haunting voice of Ethan could no longer be heard.

"It's okay. It's just me and you. I got you," Eugene said soothingly.

Ryan believed him.

***

Ryan hasn't gotten his rut after Ethan's death. Mateless wolves never usually had the urge to breed, so it was natural. Or so he thought until he was hit with one.

That week, Aron was with his parents. They were spending weekends with him to ensure he grew independent and wasn't always dependent on Eugene.

When Ryan arrived home, his plan was to slip into his bedroom unnoticed. However, it was Eugene who greeted him at the door for some reason that day.

Mine, his wolf had growled, and the next thing he knew, he pulled Eugene into a breathtaking kiss. Eugene smelled heavenly and tasted even better. He didn't think twice before slipping his tongue into Eugene's mouth and devouring him.

The Omega melted against his chest, fisting his shirt and pulling him closer. His moans drove Ryan crazy.

The alpha pulled back, staring momentarily at Eugene's swollen lips and disheveled look. He was so fucking handsome. Eugene chased his mouth with a soft whine, and Ryan lost the battle with his sanity.

Eugene. Eugene. Eugene.

Eugene filled his thoughts, and his sweet lime scent drowned him. He tasted warm and welcome. Sweet. Delicate. Addictive.

Mine. His wolf kept chanting, relishing every moan and swallowing every gasp. Eugene bloomed so beautifully under his touch.

They tangled under the sheets, each touch lingering and filled with overwhelming desire.

When the haze of rut finally cleared after days, Ryan looked at Eugene's face and felt right at home. He made love to him one last time, savoring every second. Just as he came, knotting him one last time, Ethan's face flashed in his mind.

"You broke your promise," he accused, face twisting with anger. *"He's my brother! I trusted you."*

And Ryan crumbled. "Ethan..."

I'm sorry.

I'm so sorry.

Ryan sobbed, passing out on top of Eugene. When he woke up again, Eugene was gone. The next time they came face to face, Ryan was so ashamed of losing control and overwhelmed with guilt that he couldn't meet him in the eye.

One day became two, and then three. He knew he had to bring it up, but the talk just never happened. Every time he met Eugene's eyes, he chickened out.

However, Ryan knew he needed to come to terms with this. He was an adult, and he knew exactly what he was doing. It wasn't just his rut.

His wolf wanted Eugene, and they were both in love with him. After mulling over so much and talking to his therapist, he decided it was time to let Ethan go.

Ryan sat that day with Aron, going over every photo he possessed of Ethan. He reminisced with one with a warm smile, and when he was done, he realized he didn't have any regrets.

Ethan had a good life. Ryan did everything he could as a husband, and Ethan was happy. They were happy. Every day was a new day, and he knew in his heart, there wasn't a moment he would regret. It was unfortunate Ethan was gone. Cruel and unfair.

But life has to move on. He wasn't alone anymore. Their pup needed him, and he had responsibilities.

He glanced at his pup. Aron deserved a loving parent. Living with Ethan's memories was one thing, but it was beginning to feel like he was punishing himself and those around him, especially Eugene and Aron.

Eugene was painting by the window, lost in his world. He deserved the best, and Ryan was determined to give him that.

I should let him go along with this guilt.

*****

The pain was still fresh, and visiting Ethan's grave didn't get any easier. However, unlike the other times, Ryan felt a sense of peace he never felt before. His heart ached a little less.

"Hi," he croaked, clearing his throat and taking a moment. "It's been a while," he exhaled. Ethan continued to smile in the photo, his favorite roses sitting at the foot of the grave. "I'm sorry I broke my promise to you."

The wind ruffled his hair gently, and Ryan took a few more moments to speak. The ball in his throat tightened.

"I'm in love with your brother. I wasn't supposed to fall for him, but I did. Eugene is gentle, kind and loves our Aron like his own. He's so understanding and has been a pillar by my side ever since I lost you. I was lost in the storm and thought I couldn't make it, but he found me and guided me to the light."

A few drops of tears slid down his cheeks. Admitting it aloud wasn't easy, but felt liberating. He didn't know how Eugene felt about him. He didn't know if he would accept it either.

"I can't live like this, Ethan." With a shuddering breath, he gazed at Ethan's photo. "I love you with all my heart, but I can't let you haunt me every second of the day. I have to let you go, sweetheart. I want to remember our time together with this same fondness I'm feeling right now, but the more I think, the more bitter I am about how you left everything. I'm hurting, and our pup almost didn't make it. You were too selfish, love. I need to do this for my sake and for our pup's sake."

Ryan wiped his face and took a deep breath.

"Eugene is an amazing person and a better parent to Aron than I am. I'll be happy if he would share this life with me. He gives me a reason to smile every day." He smiled at the thought. "He's so different from you. I'm learning a different thing every day, and I still feel like there's a lot I don't know about him. I'm going to ask him out properly and make this marriage real. Thank you for everything. Thank you for loving me. I hope you can understand and be happy for us as well."

He spent a few more minutes at the grave before walking away with a light heart.

***

"Mom, do you wanna tell me why Aron isn't home for the third day in a row?" Ryan asked, dropping his office bag on the couch. "We only agreed for you to have him on the weekends."

Work has been hectic these past few months, and he could barely catch a breather. Thanks to Eugene, he didn't have to worry about his pup. However, learning that his parents were taking Aron even during weekdays didn't sit well with him.

Coming home to Aron and Eugene was his usual norm. The lack of a pup in their home didn't sit well with his wolf, and he also felt Eugene was a bit down when the pup wasn't around.

His mother looked up from the magazine she was reading. "Oh, Ryan, did you have dinner? Come, I was waiting for you."

Ryan's features have hardened. "Mom, I asked you a question. He hasn't seen Eugene in three days."

His mom smiled. "It's just your dad wanted to take him out today, and he fell asleep after playing so much. We couldn't bring ourselves to wake him up." She rubbed his arm in a soothing gesture. "He's sleeping with your dad right now. It's just for a night, Ryan."

"I've heard that one before." Ryan shook his head. "He needs to be with Eugene. If you wanted him here longer, you could invite Eugene over to stay here. I'm sure he won't disagree."

His mom pursed her lips, looking like she wanted to say something but didn't.

"I'm taking him home," Ryan announced. "You can have him on weekends, as discussed. Two days maximum at a time. If you want more time, then you can ask Eugene."

"He's our grandson. Didn't know I needed his permission," she hissed.

"And he's his omega father. It doesn't hurt to let him know that you wanted another day with his pup," Ryan retorted.

He didn't wait around for her response before storming toward his father's room to fetch his son. Ryan knew his mother wasn't fond of Eugene. The twins were polar opposites. While Ethan was everything she ever wanted in a son-in-law, Eugene was not.

Eugene wasn't exactly built for social gatherings and despised being in one unless he was forced to do it. Ethan, however, was born to host parties, and during his short life, he was well-known among her friends for being a better host.

Well, his late husband thrived, being the center of attention. But Eugene wasn't like that. His mom tried to involve him more in her lifestyle, but he just wouldn't fit in. Ryan had asked her to stop doing that when he saw how uncomfortable Eugene was.

His father protested, but Ryan just told him that they would be back on the weekend. The little one stirred in his sleep, rousing with a soft whine.

"Ryan, you didn't have to wake him up," his mother argued. "Pups need to sleep as much as possible. You shouldn't do this to him. Do you know how much time it takes for him to fall asleep again?"

The pup began to cry, not fond of being disturbed from his slumber.

"Look what you did?" she hissed. "Give him to me. Now he's gonna cry all night."

Ryan moved Aron away from her. "Mom, he has an omega father who is capable of making him sleep. I don't want to hear you downplaying his role in Aron's life. We're married now. Get used to the fact that Eugene will always be Aron's father. I'll see you this weekend."

He exited his family home without another look behind him.

Aron stopped crying and settled in his seat during the ride, falling asleep with the wind whipping his face. Ryan had rolled down the windows to distract his son, and it worked.

When they arrived home, Eugene was deep asleep in his nest. However, it was his distressed scent that lingered in the room threw Ryan off. He clenched his jaw and glanced at his pup.

Eugene might not have given birth to Aron, but he was his parent through and through. Maybe more than Ryan was even capable of. He felt the guilt claw at him. He should pay more attention to him.

Without further delay, he lowered the pup beside Eugene. The Omega reached for the pup as soon as his milky scent hit his nose. Eugene embraced the pup, scenting him immediately, and his lime scent sweetened, all distress ebbing away.

Ryan sighed in relief. He didn't understand why his parents would insist on keeping Aron longer than they should when they were fully aware how the lack of scent of the omega parent would stress the pup.

Were they trying to separate them? It was true that Aron didn't need Eugene anymore. But why would they do this without discussing it with him first? Mostly with Eugene. Eugene had every right in this as much as he did.

Ryan took a deep breath. He needed to have a word with his parents about this and come clean to Eugene about his feelings. He gently carded his fingers through the Omega's hair and smiled when Eugene nuzzled into his hand in his sleep.

"I'm sorry," he whispered. "I'll be more attentive."

***

No matter how many times Ryan tried, he just couldn't bring it up to Eugene. He was never good at holding long conversations, and this made him anxious for some reason.

So after trying and spending another two weeks uselessly mulling over it, he wrote a letter to the Omega, pouring his thoughts. However, before he could give it to him, Eugene came to him with a pregnancy test result.

The sudden surge of joy hadn't been something he felt in a while. As he stared at the result, it felt just the same as when he learned about Aron's conception. While Ethan had made it a huge surprise and sent him on a treasure hunt, Eugene confronted him directly.

"I'm pregnant," he said, sliding the test result toward him. "I know this is unplanned, but I'd like to know your thoughts on this."

What should he tell him? That he's happy and barely containing his excitement? Or he didn't know if he was even allowed to celebrate just yet. What if Eugene didn't want this pup?

"I-I'd like to know your thoughts first. I..." He cleared his throat. "We could, um...if that's you want..." he drawled, uncertain of what he was exactly trying to convey.

His wolf clawed at his chest to embrace Eugene, telling him how happy they were. But was he allowed to do that? Eugene was staying far from him, and the distance was killing him.

"I think Aron would love a younger brother or sister," Eugene said fondly, and relief flooded Ryan.

"I-I'll take responsibility. I'll do my best to make this as comfortable for you as possible."

What the hell are you doing, dammit?! Just hug the fuck outta him and tell him you love him.

Eugene nodded. "Thank you, Ryan." And he was gone.

Ryan eyed the spot Eugene was standing a moment before. He went on to stand on the same spot, then glanced in the direction he disappeared with a longing he couldn't explain.

If only I had the courage.

Ryan was dumbfounded when he realized they never had the chance to speak after their rut. The letter burned holes in his pocket, and he worried it might not be the right time. So he told him he'd take responsibility and do his best to support him in this.

What kind of conversation was that? Shit. He really sucked at this.

That night, Ryan stood outside Eugene's door, for god knows how long, before giving up and walking away with slumped shoulders. Maybe he should just stick to his original plan.

***

The time came two weeks later. It was Eugene's birthday. Ryan buzzed with excitement, vowing to himself that he would make it the best birthday for him. By now, he knew what Eugene liked and did not like.

He first met Eugene to ask if he was okay with revealing the news to their family. Eugene had just shrugged. "I don't mind."

So Ryan invited both their parents to their beach home. What was the perfect way to propose to Eugene? He imagined giving him the gift he bought by the waves. Eugene loved the beach. Maybe he could arrange a romantic picnic date and then ask Eugene.

When his mom volunteered to host the party, he was only glad to let her take the reins. She was the best in it, after all. And he wanted to make it a memorable event for Eugene.

The first thing he did was to leave the letter under Eugene's pillow. He'd run into Eugene just as he was about to exit the room.

"Ryan?" Surprise flashed in his eyes.

"Oh, I...um..." Panic filled him. "I...just came to check if you were here."

"I'm here now." Eugene smiled at him, looking inquisitively.

Ryan cleared his throat, averting his face just in case his flaming cheeks were red. "I...I wanted to wish you in advance."

Eugene's scent bloomed. "Thank you."

"I hope you can enjoy this weekend."

"I will. Heard you even invited Dan. Thank you for that," Eugene smiled.

Ryan preened at the compliment. "Anything for you," his own smile grew in return. "Um...You might wanna look under the pillow. Good night."

"Huh?"

Ryan disappeared from the scene with a racing heart now that he had told Eugene where he had put the letter. Unfortunately, he wasn't aware of the fact that the butler had come to fetch Eugene with the news that Dan had arrived. And he didn't know the omegas had spent the night in Dan's room catching up.

***

Ryan was a ball of nerves the next morning. He worried if Eugene would reciprocate his feelings. He couldn't sleep a wink last night and woke early for a run to calm his nerves.

He wanted to go and check Eugene in person but held himself back. He didn't have an excuse to meet him. So he busied himself with the arrangements.

Everything was good. However, his mood soured when he saw the cake and Ethan's photo on the table.

"This wasn't what I ordered," he told his mom. "I wanted a chocolate cake. This is white forest."

This was a disaster. What the hell was this? Who dared to change his order?

"Oh, I told her to change that. Ethan hated chocolate, so we always cut his favorite white forest," Eugene's mom intervened.

The alpha stared at her, speechless. *What—*

But Eugene didn't like white forest. He loved chocolate. Before he could speak, Eugene arrived with Dan. Ryan noticed his hair first, and his mood soured even further. Did Eugene reject him? No. That can't be. Maybe he didn't have time to go for it.

You're an idiot, Ryan. How could he have gotten black dye at night?

When he calmed himself and glanced up at Eugene's face, he noticed the Omega's smile had fallen. It didn't reach his eyes anymore. Guilt gnawed at his gut. This wasn't how he envisioned this party to go. He wanted Eugene happy.

"Come on, let's cut the cake," Eugene's mom chirped.

They started before he was even ready to sing. Fortunately, they sang both Eugene and Ethan's names. Ryan shoved his rising anger and frustration aside to go with the flow. He needed to talk with everyone involved, but first, he needed to know how Eugene felt about him.

When he went to Eugene's room later, he wasn't there, and the butler told him he'd gone to the beach with his best friend. So Ryan let him be. He could always talk to him later. But once again, Eugene ended up in Dan's room with no clue of the letter, waiting for him under his pillow.

***

"Hey, baby, want another bite?" He cooed at his pup, flicking his gaze to the entrance of the dining hall every few minutes. Eugene was late for breakfast, and Dan wasn't there either.

He was nervous. Did Eugene read his letter? He was pushing his food around, shifting in his seat, and lost in his thoughts.

"What happened to your hair?!"

"Why did you do this?"

"Just missed my original color."

Ryan glanced up and froze in his seat. Eugene was stunningly gorgeous, and his hair was black. He forgot how to breathe; he couldn't tear his gaze away even if he wanted to.

It was he who asked Eugene to consider dyeing his hair black, but he sure wasn't ready for the results. The Omega took his breath away, and he didn't know how to react. He knew he was staring but couldn't do anything about it.

"I preferred silver," his mom said, bringing him out of his stupor. *What? Why?*

Eugene was silent while Ryan frowned. What was wrong with them? Eugene looked great in black. In fact, Ryan couldn't get enough. It was already hard to keep his eyes off him.

Aron was fussing in his lap, and the pup turned away when Eugene tried to kiss him. It was almost comical. He wished he could record the confused pup's reaction. Aron would glance at Eugene with a confused look but cling to him if Eugene tried to engage with him.

It was even cute. He wanted to see how Aron would react when he finally realized it was indeed his omega father. He chuckled at the thought.

But more than anything, he was buzzing with excitement. He couldn't wait to get Eugene alone. He dyed his hair black. It meant he read his letter, right? The answer must be yes.

What would he tell him? Thank you? Or should he kiss him first?

His wolf shivered with delight. He couldn't wait to hug the Omega to his heart's content. But once again, Eugene left with Dan after breakfast, leaving him behind. He understood it was because they hadn't met in so long. Ryan wanted to give them space and time to catch up. But he was growing restless.

Eugene was gone the entire day, and Ryan waited for him to come home. At night, when he learned Eugene was back, he went in search of the Omega and came across his mom and Eugene's mom talking excitedly.

He paused when he heard they were talking about his pups. Then, the conversation switched to their unborn pup. He smiled, knowing finally they all had a reason to rejoice. Another member would join their family soon. He literally couldn't wait to spoil Eugene. He was going to turn away when he heard it.

"I wish this pup was an omega. He or she would look just like my Ethan. It's like Ethan himself is going to be born again, don't you think?"

Ryan's scent immediately soured. *What the hell!* Why would they want the pup to look like Ethan? What did he have to do with any of this?

He stormed inside, a growl lodged in his throat. "I'd appreciate it if you could stop bringing Ethan into every conversation," he grunted.

"Ryan?" They both jumped to their feet.

"Son, we were just talking," his mom said, pushing her hair behind her ear. "It's nothing serious."

Ryan scoffed. "Eugene is the one carrying this pup. Did you even think how he would feel if you wanted the pup to look like someone who isn't the parent?" he snarled.

His wolf despised the idea of mere comparison. Ethan already left a piece of him back, and that was Aron. Ryan didn't care whether or not Aron looked like Ethan, but he was their pup. Why would they want another pup to look like him?

His mom was the first to move. "Ryan, listen, she was just excited. The thought of him reborn as your pup is consoling to her."

"But it is punishing to me," he growled, shrugging off her hand from him. He glared at Eugene's mom, who stared at him with her mouth ajar. "You changed the cake without even asking me first, and then you went on to comment on his hair. I don't like it."

"But Ethan loves—"

"Eugene is the one celebrating his birthday now. Not Ethan. Ethan can't fucking eat that cake!" he thundered.

"Ryan!"

His mother shriveled under the hot glare he threw in her direction. "I'd appreciate it if you stop comparing my mate with my late husband, mom. Eugene looks great in black. I wanted to see him in black. In the future, keep your thoughts to yourself if you have nothing nice to offer."

"So you don't love Ethan anymore?" Eugene's mom whispered. "B-But he loved you so much."

"Ethan is dead!" Ryan hissed. "He's fucking gone and never coming back. There's a reason we bury the dead, and some things should stay buried. Just like him. My love for Ethan has nothing to do with this. I wish you could stop trying to bring him up in every fucking conversation and make this all about him, Mrs. Sanchez." His chest heaved, and he was too furious to care anymore. "If I had known, I wouldn't have invited you over," he said, panting, and shaking his head while he tried control his anger. "I just wanted to give him a

memorable birthday and celebrate the new pup. But you ruined it all."
He clenched his fists.

"Honey, I know you're hurt, but there's nothing wrong with wanting to remember Ethan on his birthday," his mother said in a pacifying tone. "She's his mother. It's natural to miss him."

"But it's wrong to make this entire thing about Ethan as if Eugene doesn't exist," Jungkook replied hotly. "I just want to remember Ethan for the good things, but you guys are tainting my memory of him with your actions. Open your fucking eyes and see what you're doing to me. To us. If you're thinking this is helping, you're wrong. I just want to live one more day without this staggering pain pulling me down. I just want to be able to breathe without this guilt clawing at me. I just want to..." His breath sawed out. "I just want to love Eugene the way he deserves." He began to walk backward. "You don't deserve Eugene. You've hurt him enough. We'll leave this place the first thing tomorrow."

He stormed away without waiting for any of their excuses. That night, once again, he couldn't find Eugene in his bedroom. So he went to Dan's room only to be told by a staff member that they had gone outside.

Ryan went to grab his pup from his grandfathers despite their protests. He was angry with himself for not saying something sooner. He thought he was sparing their feelings, but he was wrong. He would be doomed if he allowed them to do this to Eugene again.

With a sigh, he decided to wait for Eugene to come home, falling asleep with Aron in his arms and not foreseeing the chaos that was going to wake him in the morning. The letter he wrote for his husband stayed untouched under Eugene's pillow.

***

Dear Eugene,

It's me. Ryan. It's weird trying to write everything I have going on in my head, but I'm afraid I'll screw this up if I try to talk like every other time I tried. So, I've decided to articulate my thoughts here in this paper.

I don't know where to begin or how to explain. I could say 'I like you', but I don't think those three words would encompass everything I feel for you.

You're not intimidating per se, but for some reason, you leave me tongue-tied whenever I'm around you. It was never this way with Ethan, so I'm not sure how to react. I mean, he always initiates the conversations, and it was easy to follow along. But with you, I don't know how or where to begin, and I'm left conflicted with hundreds of 'what ifs.'

First of all, I'll begin by saying how grateful I am to you and everything you have done for me and Aron. In a world where even one's own blood doesn't care for the other, you stepped in to fill the shoes that were too big for you.

Eugene, I've known your brother enough to know if the roles were to reverse, he wouldn't have done it. You're selfless and kind. It still leaves me in awe whenever I see you. You don't love Aron as your responsibility. I know you love him as your own. Oftentimes, I wonder how it is even possible to have such a big heart.

After losing Ethan, I really didn't think there was another chance for me in this life. Everything became gray, and nothing mattered except for Aron. I didn't think I was capable of smiling again. But six months later, I found myself laughing with you, and for the first time, my heart felt light.

You dedicated your life for Aron and took care of him in every way possible. You were there for him in more ways than I ever was. You filled my shoes, playing the role of both parents, which was honestly something I could have never done. Eugene, you're a better father to him than me.

Initially, I couldn't bring myself to look at you because you reminded me so much of him and what I lost. You were a constant reminder of what he used to be. But as I got to know you, I realized how wrong I was.

I used to see you and wonder why your smile isn't like his smile. Why are your voices and tones different? Why wasn't it the same? I guess, at first, in the state of grief, I wanted to see him in you, or my wolf did. But it wasn't right because you weren't the same.

There's nothing similar between you both except for your appearances. But even so, I began to notice you had cute freckles that looked like constellations. You didn't like to cover them with make up like Ethan. His eyes didn't form half crescents, or his smiles sound like the beautiful jingle of bells.

You're loud, effortlessly funny, and everything Ethan never was. I didn't mean to compare, but I'm saying this because I wanted to tell you that I know the real you. You're both not the same, and I want you to know I began to fall for you because you were you.

I'm not good with my words, and I'm not sure how much I was able to convey through this.

I have feelings for you that go beyond the dynamics we have going on now. For the past few months, I've been craving for more, and now that I know what it feels like to be with you, I'm longing for more.

Eugene, thank you for spending my rut with me. It was special, but I'm sorry for being a coward. It felt like I was finally where I should be in my life.

But there's something I must tell you. Your brother once made me promise that I'd never look at another, even if he died. I don't know why he would make me promise such a thing. He was possessive, and it sounded silly at that time. I never dreamed of losing him.

After his death, I'd often dream of him, and recently, I've been flooded with guilt. I kept asking myself if this was the right thing to do. You're my husband, but you're also my late husband's brother. I couldn't bring myself to talk to you without sorting my feelings first.

You know how widowed wolves don't go through ruts, but I guess it was a sign that I was healing. Is it too much to ask for a chance with you? Is it wrong for wanting to heal and move on? Did I move on too soon?

I'm sorry if you feel like I'm trying to tie you to myself and Aron. It's never like that. I have come to genuinely admire you and want everything you have to offer. I'd understand if you don't feel the same. I'll respect your choice.

I don't think the love I had for Ethan has changed because he isn't here anymore. He will always be a part of my life and will be cherished in my memories. But I'm also in love with you, and I have realized it has nothing to do with who you were to Ethan or that you were his brother.

Maybe I'd have fallen in love with you even if you weren't his brother or looked different. It wouldn't matter. Because it's you. You matter to me.

I love you because I have witnessed how beautiful you're inside out. I have experienced the warmth of your heart, and maybe I'm selfish in this regard. I want to be the only one on the receiving end of your love and affection for the rest of our lives.

You gave me so much during the few days we were intimate. Even in that haze of my rut, I was so sure, you were in love with me or at least it felt that way whenever you whispered my name. Is it okay to hope you also somewhat feel the same way about me?

I've been writing this letter for the past two weeks. Yesterday, I came home to see you sleeping with Aron in the living room. It was then I realized I could have this for the rest of my life. And maybe I could be selfish this once.

I fear someday you'd decide you don't want to be a part of any of this and walk away. Or a day would come where Aron won't need your presence anymore, and this arrangement would come to an end. What would I do then? It hurts me to even think that's a possibility.

Eugene, I don't want to come home and not see you there. The thought alone makes me panic.

You give me reason to wake up every day and keep going. You give me several reasons to smile. These past two years have been harder on you than anyone else. I wish I could become the reason behind your smile too.

Once again, I'm a coward. So I'm gonna drop this letter somewhere you could find. Please don't hate me if this is not the future you have in mind. I'll understand.

Eugene Sanchez, would you consider making this marriage real? Will you be my husband?

P.S: I miss your natural hair and the real you I met for the first time. I saw the old photos and thought you looked stunning. Do you think you could change your hair color back to your natural ones for me? It's totally up to you. But yeah... If you changed your hair color after reading this, I'd take your answer is yes. I'm sorry if it's too cheesy. It's just...I really wish we could start fresh. We are already a better team. Do you think we would make a great couple too?

- Ryan

Chapter - 3

♥

Eugene was no stranger to pain. He wouldn't say these two years were full of pain. There were good days and bad days. But in the end, the pain just got unbearable.

Or it was all him because he'd fallen even deeper with Ryan, and his omega couldn't take it anymore. He thought putting a distance between himself and the alpha would help. However, he was more miserable than ever.

The wolf whined and howled inside of him, crying for his mate. It was sad, and Eugene was too. Dan was right beside him, holding him through it all. His best friend refused to leave his side when he wasn't working.

"Eugene, please drink this." Dan pushed a glass of fresh orange juice to his chapped lips. "You haven't eaten anything in two days. This is bad for your baby."

Eugene shook his head. He wasn't hungry. He couldn't stomach it even if he wanted to. His body rejected everything. The omega hadn't considered the consequences of leaving. It was physically hurting him at this point.

This was a phase, he told himself. It would pass. He would be fine. He just had to make it through this.

"Please," Dan pleaded. "Just take a sip. It's okay if you puke everything later. Just try for me."

Eugene twisted his face but went on to take a sip. Strangely, his stomach didn't protest yet, so he took a hesitant gulp before draining the entire glass. It was refreshing, but it smelled wrong. His body wretched with that one thought, emptying all its contents in the next moment.

Fucking sweet oranges.

He dry heaved, body racking with more waves, but Dan was there to hold him so he didn't curl on the floor like he wanted to. His friend picked him up and carried him to the bathroom, helping him clean and rubbing his back while he cried.

"I fucking hate oranges now." He plopped on the lid of the toilet bowl, dropping his head between his hands.

"I'm sorry. I'll get you something else." Dan grimaced, crouching in front of him. "It slipped my mind. Sorry, bubs. I'll be careful next time. No more oranges."

Eugene felt ashamed. "I don't want to do this, but when I think it all started because of him, I'm angry with everything that's associated with him."

Dan didn't say anything but held him with a sigh.

"I miss my pup," he sniffled. "I miss him so much... Why, Dan? Why do I have to go through this?"

"I'm sorry, bubs. It's gonna be okay. You have me."

But Eugene was inconsolable, just like he was two days ago. "Ethan might have given birth to him, but I was the one who brought him up like he was mine, you know? Right from day one." He wiped his nose before grabbing a tissue to blow his nose. "He always sleeps on my chest." He gripped his chest, feeling the absence of the weight he'd gotten so used to.

Honestly, it was a surprise when Ethan announced his pregnancy. He never wanted to be a parent. Not for at least until he turned thirty. That was what his twin always told him.

"I'm not ready for that, Eugene. It's too much work. I just want to enjoy my life. Have fun and live my life every day as if it's my last. Do I look like parent material to you?"

After Aron's birth, he would just thrust the pup into Eugene's arms after nursing him and go back to his much-needed rest. After two months, when it became evident the pup was getting attached to Eugene more than Ethan, Ryan's mother intervened, sending Eugene home despite Ethan's protests.

His brother had complained non-stop about how much of a work everything was. Ryan had finally hired a nanny only two days before Ethan's death. Ethan had gushed to him that he was finally free to enjoy his life the way he wanted. Only his excitement didn't last.

Eugene's omega was attached to his nephew from his birth. Perhaps that was the reason he stepped up to the role without second thoughts. He just hadn't thought how hard it would be to walk away when the time came.

Ryan promised to let him walk away, but he didn't promise that he would protect his heart.

Why were you so easy to love? Why did you have to be nice? Why did you have to treat me so well? Just why?

Ryan Miller, the most handsome alpha with his easygoing nature, calm smiles, comforting scent and assuring presence. Eugene's chest ached.

I miss him.

Even being in the same room as him was enough. Now, the lack of his presence was heavy in his heart. *I should have stayed despite the hurt.* But that was an easy way out. He'd be continuing to pawn his self-respect and dignity by doing so.

"You did the right thing by walking out, bubs. What they did was horrible. They always bought you white forest cake for your birthdays just because Ethan liked it. It was the same with toys, clothes, and everything else. You always settled for the second best. I won't let you do that anymore."

Ethan was a poster child. The only parents would be proud to show around, and Eugene was the problem child.

Eugene smiled sadly. "I was born second and always ended up as everyone's second choice. What's new?"

He glanced away from the mirror, feeling consoled upon seeing his natural black hair. For the first time in two years, he felt some sense of belonging, and he didn't see a stranger staring back at him.

"I hope Ryan realizes what he is missing," Dan grunted.

"I don't want him to realize anything." Eugene glanced at his hands. "I'll still be the second best to him."

"Eugene..."

Ryan hadn't fallen in love with him in the past two years. What was going to change in a matter of two days? Does it even matter anymore? He walked out. End of the story.

Eugene stood. "I'm sorry. I can't do this." He stormed to the room with another sob bubbling in his throat. Only his mouth said he didn't care, but his heart longed for the alpha. Was it too much to ask?

A part of him yearned for Ryan to come in search of him. Would Ryan even care? Eugene didn't want to know the answer to that question. It'd break him if Ryan didn't show up, but it'd also prove why he did the right thing by walking out.

Maybe he shouldn't have developed hope or even dreamed of a day when Ryan would look at him differently. Eugene was the only one to be blamed because Ryan told him from the beginning that he couldn't give him what he wanted. But he'd fallen deeper and deeper until there was no escape from an alpha who didn't share the same sentiment.

Oh, how much he wished he could drown his sorrows in a drink. Or just take something that would help him sleep it off. But with the pup, he couldn't do anything.

It hurt even more to think that this pup would have to grow without knowing the love or affection of its alpha father. *You knew this would happen.* It was a small price to pay. If he stayed, he didn't think he would be able to make it much longer.

He had already lost sight of who he was. The omega couldn't afford to lose anymore. There was nothing left to lose. Even his heart was broken into pieces.

Eugene curled into a ball under the sheets, already missing his nest back at home. His wolf whimpered. Did he even have a home anymore? What was the point in building a nest without his alpha's scent in it?

Dan could only watch helplessly as his friend fell into a fitful sleep, letting out soft whimpers every now and then.

***

Two days ago.

Ryan didn't know when or how he fell asleep. But he was woken up with an urgent shake on his shoulders by his butler. Aron stirred from his sleep and fussed a little bit from where he slept on his chest.

"Master Miller, wake up. You must come right now."

Ryan blinked wearily, running a hand down his face. "What happened?" The urgency in his butler's tone was unsettling, and it brought an unpleasant feeling.

"It's Mr. Sanchez. He…He's gone."

"What?" Ryan sat upright, startling the pup. Aron let out a whimper, and he patted his back on instinct. "What the fuck do you mean he's gone?" he growled, lowering his voice, but at the same time, one arm shot forward to grab the butler by his collar to shake him.

Aron started crying as if sensing his anger and concern. His wolf surged forward with those two words repeating in his mind. Eugene was home last night. He had nothing good to associate with those two words.

"He left a letter," the butler said, face growing pale. He grabbed his hand with both of his with a pleading look. "The security said he left home a little after midnight with his suitcase."

Ryan ignored the pup's cries as he dashed down the hall to where everyone had gathered. With a racing heart, he snatched the letter from his mother's hand. His gaze landed on the neat crawls, and with every word, his heart sank deeper and deeper.

He read the small portion meant for him in the letter repeatedly. What did Eugene mean by this? He changed the hair color, didn't he? His hands trembled. Or did he misread the room?

The pup continued to cry, and his mother reached for him. "Don't," Ryan snarled, moving the pup out of her way. "What the fuck did you tell him?!"

"Ryan, language," his father growled.

Ryan growled back but did not remove his gaze from his mother. "What the fuck did you tell him?"

"Ryan, it's…we just talked," she stammered a little. "It was nothing serious."

"Did you tell him that he's here only because he looks like Ethan?" he asked, and the way she averted her gaze answered his question. "You never liked him. Now he's gone." He stepped back, glaring at every available individual with a newfound hatred and anger.

"I just told him to change his hair color because Aron wouldn't recognize him, and it made everyone uncomfortable," she reasoned. "I didn't think it was a big deal. I thought silver suited him better."

"No. You just wanted him to be Ethan," Ryan growled. "Aron is a pup. He was confused to see Eugene with a new hair color, that's all. He just needed time to get used to his new appearance. You had no right to tell him that."

"Ryan...he must be at your home. Where could he have gone?" his mom tried comforting him.

"I don't know. You tell me," he countered. "Where could he have gone? Because he's certainly not here anymore." He glared at her, and she cowered under his intense gaze.

"Ryan, I'm sorry."

Ryan shook his head, taking another step back. "I don't want to talk to you now."

"Ryan, she's your mother," his father tried to reason. "Calm down, son. He wouldn't have gone that far. He must be either at your place or in Spain."

Ryan scoffed. "You don't know him," he hissed. "He's gone, and he's never coming back."

"We will find him," his father assured him, but Ryan couldn't be consoled that easily.

"You took my only hope away from me," his voice cracked. "I'll never forgive you for this."

He began to climb the stairs, two at a time with his pup, patting his back to calm him down. Aron needed Eugene as soon as he woke up.

He didn't know how his mom handled him in the mornings, but now he had no time for that. Surely, he was in no mood to give his pup to her after learning what she said to Eugene.

He found the letter untouched under Eugene's pillow, just where he left it. His heart sank as the situation settled in. Eugene never learned how Ryan felt about him. Ryan packed his bags and left, ignoring their protests and pleading to stop.

***

Present.

Dan had been friends with Eugene and Ethan most of his life but was closer to Eugene than his twin. Unlike others, he never had trouble identifying his best friend.

The moment he saw Eugene's eyes, he knew his best friend. Maybe that was what brought them closer. There was a time when Eugene would pout and complain why no one could tell them apart. One of his best friend's pet peeves was someone calling him by his twin's name.

Eugene was naughty, while Ethan was all about appearances and reputation. His Eugene wouldn't think twice before sneaking out with him or getting involved in a prank. The omega was full of life and romantic at heart. He had so many dreams about his alpha, so many expectations. Dan was there when they met Ryan for the first time. He saw the way his best friend bloomed in the presence of the alpha and wilted shortly after when the alpha asked Ethan for a dance. That night, Dan danced with Eugene to keep him distracted while Ethan danced with the alpha, mesmerized and lost in their own world.

Dan would fight the world and wage a war if it was to protect his best friend, but how was he supposed to protect his heart? When he learned of Ethan's death and Eugene's new predicament, he opposed it as any best friend would do.

The model had felt a gnawing sensation that the family was trying to replace Ethan with his twin, using this marriage as an excuse. Eugene was the pup's uncle. He could have taken care of the pup by being their guest. Why was marriage even necessary?

Ryan was in no position to oppose or think on his own. He walked like a zombie and stared at a distance for hours in the end. The alpha was lost, and the others strung him along like a puppet.

In these two years, Dan couldn't do anything but watch as the light in Eugene's eyes dulled, and he lost the sense of who he was. The smile on his face lost its genuineness and became forced.

Life was too cruel to Eugene. Dan did everything in his power to console his best friend, but what could he do when Eugene had already imprinted on his husband and pup? His wolf and human side were grieving, and Dan could only watch helplessly.

Work was hectic, and he was exhausted, but nothing mattered to him when it came to Eugene. Dan stayed until Eugene fell into a fitful sleep and stepped out for a while.

Aimlessly, wandering the busy streets of Italy had helped him clear his mind a little bit. However, his mood changed as soon as he exited the elevator at the sight of someone he didn't expect to see.

Dan stormed toward the alpha and hissed, "What the hell are you—" His next words died in his throat when Ryan lifted his head to look at him. "You look like shit."

The alpha smiled sadly and glanced down at the pup sleeping in his arms. The pup's distressed scent infiltrated his senses. Thankfully, Ryan had the sense to use a scent blocker before coming.

With disheveled hair, two days of beard, red-rimmed eyes, and a swollen face, Ryan looked like he hadn't slept these few days.

"How did you know I'm here?" Dan asked, unlocking the door.

"I called a few friends and asked for a favor," Ryan confessed. "Eugene wasn't in Spain, so I guessed he must be with you."

Dan eyed the pup, who looked exhausted, and dried tear stains lined his chubby cheeks. His heart clenched as his paternal instincts kicked in. "Eugene doesn't wanna see you." His protest was weak.

"Just once." Ryan looked as if he was ready to beg on his knees if it came to that. Dan had seen him like this before. At Ethan's funeral. "I'll leave after I talk to him once if he still doesn't want me here."

Dan opened the door wide and stepped inside, gesturing at him with his head. "Eugene is in the bedroom. Don't make me regret this."

Relief flooded the distraught alpha's features. "I won't," he assured before hurrying to the bedroom.

Dan eyed the bags Ryan left in the corridor with a sigh. It was going to be a long night.

***

Eugene was dreaming. In his dream, his alpha and the pup came back. They were huddled in his nest, lazily scenting and snuggling. It was such a happy dream, but why does it hurt so much?

The omega woke up, sitting straight and rubbing his chest where it ached. He was so used to the pup's warmth at nights that the bed felt too cold without Aron here. Aron was the only one who anchored him to the shore throughout the storm.

Tears welled in his eyes. What was the point? Aron was never his, was he? Ryan's mother never failed to remind him whenever she came to pick him up at her will.

"He's my son's pup. He should grow up to be independent. That's our deal. But you're suffocating him to the point he can't be without you for even a minute."

It was natural for the pups to be close to their parent figure. Still, Eugene never understood why it was wrong for him to love the pup as his own. He knew he was a stand in, but Aron was just a pup. His wolf was attached to the pup and every time he had to be away from the pup hurt him physically and emotionally. But what could he do? He knew he was just a replacement parent until the pup was of age.

The door burst open, and his wolf perked when he sensed the milky scent he'd recognized from miles away. His eyes went wide like saucers, and his jaw went slack. Ryan stood in front of him, looking as if he had been through one hell of a storm.

"Ryan?"

"You left us."

Eugene's mouth opened and closed, still processing the fact that Ryan was here in person. So was the pup. His wolf greedily gulped the pup's scent, hands reaching out to hold him of its own volition.

My pup, his wolf chanted.

Ryan handed the pup to him, and the distressed scent made Eugene's heart constrict painfully. *Shit.*

He embraced the pup, holding him tight against his chest, and scented him furiously, hoping to take every ounce of distress.

My pup. My precious little bean.

"He wouldn't stop crying," Ryan continued. "He hadn't eaten anything in two days." Eugene grimaced, guilt washing over him. "I understand why you left me, but what did your pup do? You could have at least taken him with you. He's yours."

The tears Eugene had been holding back slid down his cheeks.

"I'll understand if I don't have a place in your life, but please don't punish our pup for my mistakes."

"Ryan," his voice cracked, and he couldn't meet the alpha's gaze.

"Let me speak," Ryan cut him off. "Please…" he added. "You said everything you had to say in that letter, but you never read this or stopped to hear what I had to say." The alpha thrust an envelope in his hands. "I wrote this before your birthday. I hoped you'd read this if I put it under your pillow because you have a habit of making your bed before you went to sleep. I thought you'd notice this when you fluff your pillows at night. I was mistaken."

Eugene reached for the letter with a shaky hand. His fingers trembled.

"I'll wait outside." Ryan looked as if he wanted to hug the omega. His fists clenched and unclenched by his sides. "If your decision doesn't change even after reading this, then I'll leave you be," he said in a determined voice. "But even if there's a sliver of hope, I want to take it. I'll wait forever if there's a chance." Then he pivoted on his heel, exiting the room.

Eugene stared at the closed door for a long moment and then at the sleeping pup. Aron nuzzled closer to his chest in his sleep, small fists bunching the front of his t-shirt with a soft whine, leaving his throat.

He shushed the pup, thoughts spiraling and the envelope heavy in his hand. Eugene was afraid to open and see what was inside. Did Ryan sign their divorce papers? What did he mean by another chance?

A ball of emotion lodged in his throat, and he carefully slid the paper out of the envelope. A rush of relief flooded him as soon as he saw it was just a handwritten letter. However, a new sense of foreboding filled him when he read the first line.

Dear Eugene,

It's me. Ryan. It's weird trying to write everything I have going on in my head, but I'm afraid I'll screw this up if I try to talk like every other time I tried. So, I've decided to articulate my thoughts here in this paper.

Eugene took a deep breath. Was he trying to break it off without hurting his feelings? He scolded himself for jumping ahead when he didn't know what Ryan even meant. Steeling his heart, he continued to read. He could do this.

I don't know where to begin or how to explain. I could say 'I like you', but I don't think those three words would encompass everything I feel for you.

Huh?

You're not intimidating per se, but for some reason, you leave me tongue-tied whenever I'm around you. It was never this way with Ethan, so I'm not sure how to react. I mean he always initiates the conversations, and it was easy to follow along. But with you, I don't know how or where to begin, and I'm left conflicted with hundreds of 'what ifs.'

His heart began to race for entirely different reasons this time, and his scent fluctuated, revealing how he felt. What was he trying to say?

First of all, I'll begin by saying how grateful I am to you and everything you have done for me and Aron. In a world where even one's own blood doesn't care for the other, you stepped in to fill the shoes that were too big for you.

Eugene, I've known your brother enough to know if the roles were to reverse, he wouldn't have done it. You're selfless and kind. It still leaves me in awe whenever I see you. You don't love

Aron as your responsibility. I know you love him as your own. Oftentimes, I wonder how it is even possible to have such a big heart.

Was this a letter to show his gratitude? Was this sugar-coating right before Ryan handed him a bitter pill?

After losing Ethan, I really didn't think there was another chance for me in this life. Everything became gray, and nothing mattered except for Aron. I didn't think I was capable of smiling again. But six months later, I found myself laughing with you, and for the first time, my heart felt light.

Oh.

You dedicated your life to Aron and took care of him in every way possible. You were there for him in more ways than I ever was. You filled my shoes, playing the role of both parents, which was honestly something I could have never done. Eugene, you're a better father to him than me.

Eugene choked on a sob, his tears betraying him once again. He hugged the pup to his chest. *Yes, I am. I'm a good father.* Guilt flooded him. How could he think Aron would be able to live without him? He had been too selfish, hadn't he?

Initially, I couldn't bring myself to look at you because you reminded me so much of him and what I lost. You were a constant reminder of what he used to be. But as I got to know you, I realized how wrong I was.

Eugene bit his lip. There was it—the truth. He glanced away, taking several breaths to regulate his breathing, and fought to stay strong enough to get through the rest of the letter.

I used to see you and wonder why your smile isn't like his smile. Why are your voices and tones different? Why wasn't it the same? I guess, at first, in the state of grief, I wanted to see him in you or my wolf did. But it wasn't right. Because you weren't the same.

Oh. He wasn't comparing.

There's nothing similar between you both except for your appearances. But even so, I began to notice you had cute freckles that looked like constellations. You didn't like to cover them with make up like Ethan. His eyes didn't form half crescents, or his smiles sound like the beautiful jingle of bells.

A wave of warmth rushed to his chest, and the corners of his lips twitched.

You're loud, effortlessly funny, and everything Ethan never was. I didn't mean to compare, but I'm saying this because I wanted to tell you that I know the real you. You're both not the same, and I want you to know I began to fall for you because you were you.

Heat flared in his cheeks, and Eugene took a momentary pause before re-reading the lines again. *He was falling for me?* His treacherous heart fluttered, and his wolf nudged him to read further. This time, his hand trembled for different reasons.

I'm not good with my words, and I'm not sure how much I was able to convey through this.

I have feelings for you that go beyond the dynamics we have going on now. For the past few months, I've been craving for more, and now that I know what it feels like to be with you, I'm longing for more.

Eugene gasped. Oh, my god! His jaw was slack, and his eyes popped out. There was an absolute silence around him before his thoughts came back to him in full force. *Ryan loves me. He has feelings for me. I misunderstood the entire situation.*

Eugene, thank you for spending my rut with me. It was special, but I'm sorry for being a coward. It felt like I was finally where I should be in my life.

Eugene's cheeks were aflame, and he was sure he'd look red. His scent sweetened as if someone just added a cube of sugar to fresh lime extract.

But there's something I must tell you. Your brother once made me promise that I'd never look at another, even if he died. I don't know why he would make me promise such a thing. He was possessive, and it sounded silly at that time. I never dreamed of losing him.

What? Why would he do that? Ethan had always been selfish and possessive, but Eugene didn't realize it extended to this level.

After his death, I'd often dream of him, and recently I've been flooded with guilt. I kept asking myself if this was the right thing to do. You're my husband, but you're also my late husband's brother. I couldn't bring myself to talk to you without sorting my feelings first.

He was suffering all this time, and Eugene didn't know. Shame filled him. They could have just talked, but Eugene had no one else to blame. They both had their battles to fight.

You know how widowed wolves don't go through ruts, but I guess it was a sign that I was healing. Is it too much to ask for a chance with you? Is it wrong for wanting to heal and move on? Did I move on too soon?

He vaguely remembered learning something along the lines in school, but things made more sense now. No one knew Ryan went into rut. He'd informed his mom that Ryan came down with a viral flu and asked her to keep Aron for a couple of days, which she happily agreed to.

Why wouldn't she? She was already looking for ways to separate Aron from him. Though she reasoned that it was to make the pup self-dependent, Eugene knew better.

Ryan's mother did not like him. Eugene wasn't an ideal trophy wife material like Ethan was. He wasn't a good host and didn't know a thing about organizing parties. He wasn't someone she could parade proudly among her socialite friends.

The omega sighed. It was all over now. He hoped he wouldn't have to see her again.

I'm sorry if you feel like I'm trying to tie you to myself and Aron. It's never like that. I have come to genuinely admire you and want everything you have to offer. I'd understand if you don't feel the same. I'll respect your choice.

What? *I stayed because I wanted to.* It has always been my choice.

I don't think the love I had for Ethan has changed because he isn't here anymore. He will always be a part of my life and will be cherished in my memories. But I'm also in love with you, and I have realized it has nothing to do with who you were to Ethan or that you were his brother.

Maybe I'd have fallen in love with you even if you weren't his brother or looked different. It wouldn't matter. Because it's you. You matter to me.

That's what I always wanted. Oh, god, Ryan! Why didn't he say something sooner?

I love you because I have witnessed how beautiful you're inside out. I have experienced the warmth of your heart, and maybe I'm selfish in this regard. I want to be the only one on the receiving end of your love and affection for the rest of our lives.

Eugene was crying, but his scent remained sweet. He didn't even know this letter existed because he'd been sleeping in Dan's room during their stay at Miller's mansion.

You gave me so much during the few days we were intimate. Even in that haze of my rut, I was so sure you were in love with me, or at least it felt that way whenever you whispered my name. Is it okay to hope you also somewhat feel the same way about me?

I've been writing this letter for the past two weeks. Yesterday, I came home to see you sleeping with Aron in the living room. It was then I realized I could have this for the rest of my life. And maybe I could be selfish this once.

I fear someday you'd decide you don't want to be a part of any of this and walk away. Or a day would come where Aron won't need your presence anymore, and this arrangement would come to an end. What would I do then? It hurts me to even think that's a possibility.

Eugene sniffled. Ryan was struggling himself. The alpha had so much to tell him, and Eugene misunderstood his silence for lack of love.

Eugene, I don't want to come home and not see you there. The thought alone makes me panic.

You give me reason to wake up every day and keep going. You give me several reasons to smile. These past two years have been harder on you than anyone else. I wish I could become the reason behind your smile too.

Eugene covered his mouth, sobbing into his hand so he didn't wake up Aron. Ryan and Aron were the only reason for his smiles these past two years.

Once again, I'm a coward. So I'm gonna drop this letter somewhere you could find. Please don't hate me if this is not the future you have in mind. I'll understand.

Eugene Sanchez, would you consider making this marriage real? Will you be my husband?

Oh, god! Yes, a thousand times yes. He laughed through his tears. Ryan loved him. Suddenly, things weren't so dark anymore. Everything was so bright.

P.S: I miss your natural hair and the real you I met for the first time. I saw the old photos and thought you looked stunning. Do you think you could change your hair color back to your natural ones for me? It's totally up to you. But yeah... If you changed your hair color after reading this, I'd take your answer is yes. I'm sorry if it's too cheesy. It's just...I really wish we could start fresh. We are already a better team. Do you think we would make a great couple too?

- Ryan

Shit. Ryan must have thought he changed his hair color after reading that letter. Since he couldn't believe his eyes, he read the letter once again from top to bottom. This was real. Ryan was in love with him, and he loved him for who he was, not because he looked like his twin.

Eugene took a deep breath, fighting the urge to run into Ryan's arms. As happy and relieved he was to learn this, it wasn't that easy. With a sigh, he scented the pup one more time, making him lie on the bed. The pup stirred a bit but settled soon, burying his nose into the sheets where Eugene lay earlier.

He found Ryan in the sitting area on one side of the couch, with Dan occupying the other end. His friend immediately stood, reading his face for a moment before slipping inside the bedroom.

Ryan, too, climbed to his feet, putting the cup of coffee on the table. He faced Eugene, and the omega saw the turmoil there. Eugene opened and closed his mouth, trying to find the suitable words, but failed.

"Ryan."

"Eugene."

With a soft sob, Eugene closed the distance between them. Throwing his arms around Ryan's shoulder, he pulled him closer, burying his face into his neck. The lack of scent annoyed him, but Eugene wasn't gonna complain. The alpha was here, and that was all that mattered.

The hug was everything. Ryan's embrace was just like he imagined—tight and warm. They had hugged before, but those brief hugs held nothing against the tight one Ryan gave him now. There was fear, urgency, and desperation.

One of the alphas' large hands cupped the back of his head, and the other draped over his back. He enveloped him in a full-body hug, and Eugene marveled at how they fit like a puzzle piece. It felt so right as if they were made for each other.

The omega stood on tiptoes, hooking his chin over the alpha's shoulder. All the past pain and insecurities became a thing of the past, and only Ryan remained.

The alpha's body shook, and Eugene heard the soft sniffles. If Eugene was doubtful of his decision before, now he had no doubts.

One look into Ryan's eyes, and he'd known. "I love you," he mumbled in between his sobs. "I love you so much."

"I love you too." Ryan's hands closed around him impossibly tight, and he lifted him off the ground. "I love you to the point it hurts."

"W-We need to talk," Eugene whispered. If this serenity had to last, it was important they had that delayed talk. It couldn't be put off anymore. Ryan needed to know what was going on in his mind.

"Okay." The alpha nodded. "We will talk."

"I'm sorry." Eugene shuddered. "I shouldn't have walked away like that."

He felt the alpha shaking his head. "No, you did the right thing." Ryan pulled back, and the omega missed the warmth. "I should have known what you were putting up with. I'm sorry I failed to pay close attention."

Eugene shook his head. "You didn't know. You were hurting too."

"Doesn't mean I had to be ignorant." Ryan sniffed. "I should have created an environment that made you comfortable enough to come to me if you had any issues. But I failed to give you that. You felt like you couldn't talk to me, and I'm the reason for that."

"We are equally responsible." Eugene could have talked to him. They were a great team, weren't they? But he'd disregarded his feelings for Ryan and brushed it aside. But those brushed-aside feelings had grown to an extent where it was beginning to hurt him. "You couldn't read my mind. I should have talked to you and told you something sooner."

Ryan was silent for a moment. "I'm sorry for everything. I ordered a chocolate cake for your birthday, but..." He bit his bottom lip. "I should have been more attentive. I shouldn't have let you cut that stupid cake and put my foot down. But I didn't know what to do in front of all of them. I felt disheartened to see Ethan's photo there. It felt as if they were guilt-tripping me for even trying to move on."

Eugene felt a pang in his chest. He noticed his dislike for a white forest. Ryan had known. Something warm filled his chest again. "It's okay." He glanced away, but it was futile. Ryan had a very clear view of his face.

"No, it's not," Ryan disagreed. "I didn't know your mom would cancel my order and change the flavor. I should have stopped them from celebrating Ethan's birthday from the very first year after his passing. That time, I didn't want to stop a grieving mother by saying something." His fists clenched by his side. "Now I realize I have let things go too far because I was lost in my grief. Instead of celebrating a living person, they were living with the memory of a dead person. I didn't know my mom was giving you a hard time either."

Eugene looked down. He couldn't bring himself to say it was okay this time. It wasn't. Her actions hurt more. Same with his mom. His mom should have known better, and his dad shouldn't have stayed silent.

"She always gave me reasons for keeping Aron with her during the weekdays," Ryan continued. "The last time, I fought with her and told her she wasn't allowed to do that. I don't understand why she would go behind my back to tell you things I never intended. You're not him, and I've never seen you as his replacement."

"I know."

"I'm sorry. I was so lost in my issues that I didn't notice your problems."

"It's okay."

Ryan stepped forward to take his hands in his, covering them between his large palms. "It's not, and you know it." He then held both his hands in front of his chest. "These two days were hell for me and Aron. It felt as if I lost any sense of direction and couldn't function at all. I realized I needed you like I needed air to breathe. Without you, it was suffocating."

Eugene's eyes filled with tears. "Ryan…"

The alpha's thumb caressed the back of his palm. "I love you, Eugene. I should have manned up and told you sooner. I'm sorry my lack of correspondence caused you so much pain."

Eugene leaned to press his face into the alpha's chest. "Ryan, there's something I want to tell you." He closed his eyes and took a deep breath, wishing he could have smelled the alpha if it wasn't for the scent blockers.

"Tell me."

"I can't go back." Ryan stiffened but tried to maintain his posture. "I love you, but I can't go back to that life. I can't see them... not like this. I don't want to be anywhere near them. I lost sight of who I was and became a person I didn't recognize. I can't allow them to control my life anymore." Eugene took a deep breath. "I promised myself that I'll put myself first."

Ryan cupped his face, and Eugene felt some of the tension leave his body. "Then we don't have to go back."

Eugene blinked up to look at him. The alpha's hand slid to caress his stomach.

"You, Aron, and this little one is my world. My home is wherever you are. I'm not leaving you. We will go wherever you want to go. We will start over."

A small smile tugged at the corners of his lips. Hope bloomed in his heart. "Really?"

"Really." Ryan nodded. "They don't deserve you. I don't either. I've had a gem in my hand all this time, yet I didn't see its worth until later."

"Don't say that." Eugene moved closer to the alpha again. "Don't take all the blame yourself."

Ryan closed the remaining distance to rest his forehead against his. "I know we have a long distance to go. Give me another chance to love you the right way, Eugene. Please...give me one more opportunity."

"Okay." Eugene nodded furiously, tears spilling and heart racing again. "Okay. I'll give you another chance."

"Thank you." Ryan closed his eyes. "Thank you so much."

"Did you eat?" Eugene pulled back to ask. He despised seeing the bags under the alpha's eyes and the dark circles that spoke of his restlessness.

Ryan shook his head. "Just coffee."

Eugene scowled before pulling away. "Why don't you freshen up? I'll order something."

He went to grab the phone, feeling small tugs of hunger. It was a miracle how love could change things in a matter of seconds. He hadn't wanted to eat anything a while ago, but now he was hungry. Ryan didn't argue. He trudged toward the bathroom, but his sluggish steps told him how exhausted the alpha was, physically and emotionally. Thinking about it, he'd only seen Ryan like that a handful of times.

It was a testament to how much his absence had affected the alpha. Was he an asshole for finding a weird sort of comfort from this? He'd longed for his love for so many years. Now that he finally had it, Eugene's heart was at peace.

The voice on the other end of the phone distracted him, and Eugene gathered himself to order food for all three. Once done, he went to the bedroom to see Dan curled around the pup, fast asleep. He sat at the edge of the bed, combing his fingers through the other omega's hair.

Dan had suffered, too, because of him. He sighed. Dropping a kiss on top of his pup's head, he went out to see the alpha on the couch. Ryan had discarded his jacket, wearing only his shirt and pants. He'd washed his face and combed his hair.

The alpha perked at his sight and beckoned him over, patting the empty side of the couch. Eugene obeyed with a soft smile.

"There's a lot to talk about," Eugene said, and the alpha nodded in agreement.

"We have all the time to talk now," Ryan kissed his knuckles, bringing a flush to his cheeks. "But I want to hold you first. May I?"

Eugene nodded, feeling his insides melt at that simple request. When he scooted closer to the alpha and swallowed in a tight embrace with the alpha's nose buried into his hair, everything felt right. It felt as if he could win the world as long as he had Ryan.

As time passed, Ryan's scent blockers began to wane, and his patchouli scent seeped out. Eugene sank into his embrace further, melting into him. This was what he wanted. No, what he needed.

"I love you," Ryan whispered, kissing the top of his head.

Eugene smiled, feeling the heaviness and the sorrow lifting off him completely.

Love you more.

Epilogue

Two years later.

The ocean had a strange way of comforting one's heart. Two years ago, one evening, Eugene sat on a beach with a heavy heart. At that time, he'd felt as if he was met at a crossroads. He chose to prioritize himself for the first time in his life.

But then, Ryan had followed him. They'd gone to therapy individually and as a couple after they reunited and decided to give it another chance. Now, two years later, here he was with his favorite people in the world.

Ryan held their daughter Aria on his shoulders as they played tag with the waves. Her excited squeals matched his husband's laughter. Dan and his boyfriend of six months, Christopher, held Aron's hands. Their contagious laughter echoed around him.

Once upon a time, he would look at Ryan and feel uncertain about his feelings. He'd wonder if Ryan would ever look at him the same way he looked at Ryan. But now, he knew what it felt like to love and be loved in return.

Ryan showered him with so much love that he always felt so cherished. Eugene didn't know it was possible to experience this much love for a person. The alpha always prioritized him and their pups before anything else, and that was all that mattered.

With a soft smile, he caressed his abdomen, where another life grew inside of him. Life had brought unexpected changes in these two years, and he was happier than ever. Ryan was the best husband he could ever ask for.

They moved to Spain and started a new life in Seoul. Ryan quit his family business and found a good-paying job with his experience. Eugene, too, started pursuing his interest in art, taking extra courses to hone his craft.

Fortunately, after the first few months, their family stopped bothering them and trying to reconcile their differences. They had accepted they wouldn't be able to force their way into their lives.

Eugene didn't know how long it would take to forgive them and move on. However, he wasn't forcing it. He'd meet them when he was ready.

Ryan turned to meet his gaze, and Eugene waved with a smile. His husband handed their daughter to Dan and jogged toward him.

"Hey, love, wanna dip your feet?" he asked once he was near.

Eugene shook his head. "No, I'm good," he replied.

Ryan dropped beside him on the picnic blanket, supporting himself on his elbow. "I missed this." He grinned, turning to watch their children playing with Christopher and Dan. "We should do this often."

"We should," Eugene agreed. However, Ryan's work was demanding, so getting away from Seoul wasn't easy. They did manage small trips once in a while, but not much. It was a small price to pay for their freedom.

The wind blew Ryan's hair. His husband was growing it out, and it had now reached his ears. He thought long hair suited Ryan better.

It was also so soft and wavy that he loved playing with those luscious locks.

Eugene reached out to comb his fingers through his husband's hair, caressing the silky strands. "I love your hair," he confessed.

"Yeah?" Ryan's smile turned smug, his gaze suggestive. "I had a feeling with how much you love pulling my hair when we make out or mmph—"

Eugene covered his mouth. "Shut up," he hissed.

Ryan grabbed his wrist. "Shy again?" he teased, leaning forward to smack a kiss on his lips. "We literally made another pup, and you're still shy, hmm?"

"Doesn't mean I have to air these things in public," he chastised, a pink flush coating his cheeks.

Ryan chuckled, kissing his flaming cheek. "You're gorgeous when you blush."

"You always say that." He pushed at him playfully, fighting the smile tugging his lips.

"That's enough, love birds. Keep it PG!" A familiar voice pulled them out of their bubble.

Eugene glanced up to see Dan and Christopher return with the children.

"Dada!" Aron ran to him at a breakneck speed, but Ryan caught him in the middle before he could get anywhere near him.

"Not that fast, pup. You can't jump on Dada like that, remember?" he chided gently.

"Sorry, Papa."

Ryan kissed his nose. "Come on. Sit beside your Dada and show him what you found."

Aron launched into his tale with childish enthusiasm, showing him the shells he collected that evening and telling him the story behind each shell.

Two years ago, Eugene wouldn't have thought this evening was possible. But life was full of surprises.

Later, when Ryan held a hand for him to take, carefully lifting him up and helping him pack their stuff, he knew this was his life for a long time to come. He no longer had to yearn for love. His love was walking right in front of him, holding their pup in one arm and a picnic basket in another.

Bonus and Extended Epilogue

♥

***M**orning after their reunion*

Eugene hurried to the bedroom upon hearing Aron's cries and Dan sleepily trying to comfort the distressed pup. He slept with Ryan on the couch and woke up only when he heard Aron.

"Hey, sweetheart," he greeted and took the pup from Dan, allowing him to go back to sleep. "Did my baby get scared?" he cooed, bouncing the two-year-old in his arms. "Dada is here now." He walked out of the room with the pup in his arms.

Aron clung to him, nuzzling into his neck and finding his scent gland immediately. The pup closed his mouth over his scent gland, sucking on his skin as a form of greeting, but his whimpers didn't stop. His scent fluctuated with anger, sadness, and fear. It tugged at Eugene's heart.

Guilt filled him as he released calming pheromones to calm the pup. He'd been too selfish. Out of everyone, he felt sorry for the pup most.

He thought Aron wouldn't need him anymore. How wrong he was. Now, with Aron in his arms, he finally felt complete.

Eugene had never broken a promise intentionally, but with Aron, he did that for the first time. How was he better than Ethan? What right did he have to blame his brother when he did the same thing?

His wolf urged him to scent the pup, hold him tighter, and never let go. "I'm sorry I left like that," Eugene apologized. "I'll never leave again. I'm so sorry. I won't break my promise again." He kissed the top of the pup's head and continued to sway with him until the pup stopped whimpering.

Aron's knuckles turned white with how tight he was gripping the front of his t-shirt. Ryan, who sat up from the couch, rubbing his weary eyes, smiled softly.

Eugene sighed in relief. "I was afraid he'd reject me again," he admitted as he went to sit on the couch beside Ryan.

"He never rejected you." Ryan's voice was soft. "He was just confused after seeing you in a new hair color," he said, dropping a kiss on his shoulder and draping an arm around him. "Just wait until he gets a good look at your face and a whiff of your scent."

Just as he mentioned, Aron finally lifted his head to see Eugene, and the pup froze. Eugene, too, stiffened, wondering what would happen next. Several emotions crossed the pup's features before his lips began to tremble. He glanced at Ryan, letting out a cry.

"What is it, sweetheart?" Ryan cooed.

Aron stopped crying and glanced at Eugene again. His lips once again trembled, and he cried again, looking at Ryan as if he were complaining about something.

"What is it, Aron? Are you confused?" Eugene asked, internally fearing another rejection, but the pup continued to glance between him and his alpha father. "It's me, pup. I'm your Dada."

The pup perked at the sound of his voice, but his face crumbled when he saw Eugene's hair.

"Pa-Pa-Pa-Pa," the pup babbled.

"Hey, baby, isn't Dada so pretty in this new hair?" Ryan poked his nose. "Look at your Dada. Doesn't black suit him better?"

Aron, however, was inconsolable for a while.

"Oh, he's such a whiner," Ryan teased.

He continued to blubber as he grabbed a fistful of Eugene's hair and tugged. For a moment, the pup seemed lost. He stopped weeping to examine his hair, but once again, confusion washed over him. He let out another cry as a form of complaint to Ryan, drawing chuckles from both his parents.

Ryan kissed Eugene's cheeks. "Told you. He's just confused and a little bit upset with the new change. He's never seen you with black hair." He hugged Eugene from the back, scooting closer to him on the couch, and Eugene blushed at their closeness. "He'll come around and see what I see," he whispered.

The omega nodded. Dan came outside right then. "Ah, the love-birds are here. I heard everything that's going on with the pup," he announced. "Let me test something," he said and tried to take Aron from Eugene.

The pup screamed, kicking his feet, but didn't let go of his grip on Eugene. Dan let go, and Aron buried his face into Eugene's chest, turning his head to scowl at his uncle.

"See," Dan pointed at the pup. "He doesn't wanna let go. Stop worrying your pretty head, Eugene."

Eugene relaxed a bit, letting out a relieved sigh. Aron didn't reject him. The pup was just confused and had to get used to his new appearance. It all lasted for thirty minutes before the pup accepted it and settled on his chest.

By the time they finished breakfast, Aron was playing with his hair with a newfound interest and refused to part with him even when he said he wanted to shower. The omega smiled, glancing at Ryan, who was watching him fondly.

As he looked at his alpha, he realized how much a proper communication could solve. They'd wasted a lot of time by overthinking and assuming stuff about each other. If they had only talked sooner...

Eugene inhaled, deciding he'd communicate with the alpha, no matter how hard the said communication was. Determination steeled his resolve. Now that he knew Ryan was in love with him, he was going to fight for them both with everything he had.

He carried the pup to the bathroom, putting him on the bathroom counter. The omega understood they had a long way to go, and their problems hadn't ended yet. But now he had every reason not to give up.

"I'm sorry for giving up, pup," he whispered. "I promise I'll never stop fighting for us."

Aron babbled something unintelligible, and Eugene could only make out words like 'Dada' and 'pwetty' that brought a smile to his face.

"Yeah? You think Dada is pretty?"

"Pwetty," the pup repeated, bouncing on his bum. The rest of the worries that were gnawing at him vanished when the pup cupped his face with his small hands, smacking a very wet kiss on his nose with an excited squeal.

Eugene knew right then things were going to be okay.

***

Two years later.

Eugene returned from the parlor. He loved getting his hair done, and after two years, he once again changed his hair color to blond. The omega loved this new look on him. It had been a while since he went blond.

He rang the bell to announce he was home before opening the door, and Aron was already at the door to greet him. The pup was now four years old and the most adorable ever.

The pup gasped at the sight of him before him and squealed, "Wow! You're so beautiful." He shifted in his feet with a bounce in his steps, face breaking into a wide grin with a mixture of awe and joy.

"Really?" Eugene bent to kiss his head.

"You look so handsome. Gorgeous." Those were the words he learned from his Papa. The pup hugged his knees with another happy squeal, looking more excited than ever. He looked as if he couldn't believe his eyes.

"Thank you, sweetheart."

Eugene went further inside to see his husband holding their two-year-old daughter, who was suckling on her pacifier. Aria looked stunned, while Ryan looked smitten. She grinned with her pacifier dangerously clinging to her mouth.

"You look so good," Ryan gushed, opening his free arm for a hug. "I love this hair on you."

"Thank you." Eugene beamed, feeling the heat in his cheeks. Nothing has changed, and he still bloomed under the alpha's praises.

"Whoa! You're hot, baby." Ryan leaned forward to kiss his lips, following it up with a few consecutive kisses. "My hot Dada."

"Hot Dada!" The pup piped in. "I have a hot Dada."

Ryan bounced Aria on his hip. "Aria, darling, look at your Dada. Isn't he the hottest Dada?"

"Yes, hot Dada. Hot Dada," Aron chimed.

Ryan chuckled while Eugene rolled his eyes. Their pup was at an age where he copied everything his alpha father did, so it was no surprise he would copy this.

"See, our pup agrees."

"Shut up." Eugene kissed him again, happiness bubbling in his chest.

"No can do. I gotta sing your praises all day. I got the hottest mate and—"

Eugene shut him up with another kiss only to feel a third presence when their daughter, who had ditched her pacifier, smacked a wet kiss on their cheeks. With Aron hugging their knees with a giggle, chanting 'hot dada' was heaven on earth for the omega.

"I love you." Ryan smiled against his lips.

Eugene saw his entire universe in his husband's eyes and thought how fortunate he was to have such a loving family. "Love you more."

Acknowledgements

Thank you for reading this work. I was planning to publish this last year but unforeseen health issues had forced me to push it back. I'm glad I was able to get it out now. Hope you had enjoyed this read.

See you soon with my next book.

For more info keep an eye on: www.cjcollinsofficial.comI'm also on X: @cjcollinshere

About the author

C. J. Collins is a lover of love. Collins celebrates love in all forms and believes it transcends gender, race, ethnicity and boundaries. Personally, Collins is an introvert until the vibe matches with a penchant for humor and sarcasm. Collins enjoys every little things life has to offer and believes life offers second chances to everyone who wish to take it.

Also by

A Night with Carters

Don't Leave Me

Love Me